SPIRITFEATHER

Colin Greenland was born in 1954 and took a D.Phil. in SF at Oxford. He won the Arthur C. Clarke award for his novel *Take Back Plenty* (1990) and is one of the pre-eminent SF writers of his generation. He lives in Cambridge with his partner, Susanna Clarke.

DREAMTIME

SPIRITFEATHER

COLIN GREENLAND

A Dolphin
Paperback

First published in Great Britain in 2000
as a Dolphin paperback
by Orion Children's Books
a division of the Orion Publishing Group Ltd
Orion House
5 Upper St Martin's Lane
London
WC2H 9EA

A catalogue record for this book
is available from the British Library.

Typeset at The Spartan Press Ltd,
Lymington, Hants
Printed in Great Britain by
Clays Ltd, St Ives plc

ISBN 1 85881 710 2

Chapter 1

Roshana Kemal is walking along a road.

She is alone. She sees no cars, no people, no animals. There aren't even any flies. There is nothing but grass, tall grass, on both sides of the road.

The sun is high in the sky. It must be time for Roshana to be at school, the School of the Blessed Nativity in Constitution Road. She doesn't know why she isn't there. She has no idea where she is.

There is nothing to do but keep walking.

The grass is thick and green, as if the rainy season has come and gone. In the distance are long low smudges of a darker green. They must be the hills, which are a long way off, yet now Roshana can feel the road rising beneath her, as if she is among them already. It's hard walking. The hill must be steep.

When she looks down, Roshana sees a tiny building. School, she thinks, though Blessed Nativity is grey and low, with a corrugated iron roof, and this is more like someone's house, big and white, with green tiles. Blessed Nativity has an asphalt playground, and this has a garden and palm trees. The garden has a dog in it. When it sees Roshana, the dog jumps up.

Roshana doesn't like dogs. She knows the dog is going to jump right up the hill and crash into her. She tries to run, but she can't. She can't feel her legs at all. She is walking as fast as she can, but moving very slowly. It is like walking in the river, against the current.

The dog howls.

The road is very small now, like a model road, a line scratched through the grass with a stick. Roshana must have grown ten times taller; or perhaps she is flying, high overhead, following the road.

The road forks. You have to choose which way to go.

Roshana doesn't want to go either way. She would turn back now, if it weren't for the dog. Anyway, she has to keep going. She must get—

She must get to—

She must get *somewhere*. She can't remember where.

At the fork in the road, someone is waiting.

It's a man. She is sure of that, though she can only see his shape, a silhouette against the sun. It is a man in a long skirt with a big turban on his head. He is standing there with his arms folded, watching Roshana come towards him.

Roshana stops. The river drags at her skirt, tugging her backwards. It will drag her back to the place where the dog is howling.

The man lifts up his hand. She thinks he is beckoning her. He will protect her from the dog.

Roshana doesn't want to go to him. She can't remember who he is.

Chapter 2

Roshana wakes. Above her head the sun is bright through the scratched plastic window. She remembers nothing of her dream.

Jino is having his breakfast. She can hear him singing and burbling happily. Her mother is coaxing him to eat another spoonful of ragi, and another.

'Swallow it, Jino, don't blow bubbles in it! That's the way. What a good little boy . . .'

Roshana stretches. She pushes off the thin sheet that covers her.

Her mother calls through the curtain. 'Roshi, are you awake there?'

'Yes, Amma.' In the caravan it is impossible to make a move without everyone knowing.

Roshana yawns. She wriggles, and lifts her legs right up in the air. She wishes she wasn't so thin. Everybody's fatter than her: Amma, Parvati, Jeevamani . . .

'Are you getting up, Roshana?'

That is a typical mother sort of question. You are not allowed to say no, even if it's the truth.

Roshana puts her feet on the floor. 'Getting up, Amma.'

She reaches for her uniform, her clean white short-sleeved blouse and blue pinafore dress that hang on a hook on the wall. While she puts them on she looks as she always does at the photo on the wall by the hook, the one of all of them, Roshana and Appa and Amma, in the meadow under the trees.

Roshana finds her bag of things and pulls out her mirror. Her brown eyes peer back at her: one, and then the other. The mirror is only big enough for one eye at a time. She gets out her hairbrush. With one hand she starts brushing her thick black hair. With the other she tucks up the curtain, which is only an old sheet hung from the ceiling.

Jino is on Amma's lap. He is happy to see her. 'Rosha! Rosha! Rosha!' he sings. He holds up his arms.

Roshana bends down to pick him up. Amma lets her, though she is still trying to give him his breakfast.

Jino reaches for Roshana's hairbrush. 'No no,' she says, tickling his round tummy. She tosses the hairbrush out of reach, into a chair.

'What a mess, Roshi,' says Mrs Kemal, winding her fingers into her daughter's hair. 'No one would think I braided this for you yesterday.'

The little caravan is hot. Flies roam around. Jyoti Kemal tidies her daughter's hair and spoons her son's breakfast into his mouth at the same time. Somehow she manages to do both perfectly well.

'Where have you been in the night to get this so tangled? Running through the jungle?'

Her own hair is as thick and black as Roshana's, and long enough to sit on when she lets it down. Roshana can't remember the last time she saw Amma with her hair down.

Roshana has her breakfast: a big mug of tea and a chapatti with chutney. She licks the chutney spoon.

'Now, Roshi, is there anything you have to take to school today?'

'Oh yes. My book.'

Roshana looks for the book. She looks on the floor around her bed. She sees a black feather lying there.

She picks up the feather and examines it. It is clean and shiny, as if freshly fallen.

'Amma?' she says. 'Was there a bird in here?'

'What?' says her mother. She is getting Jino into his jacket. 'Other arm. No, nuisance, *other* arm!'

Roshana twirls the stem of the feather between her thumb and finger. She looks out of the window. She sees a pile of crates and a brick wall.

The caravan stands at the bottom of the yard of Mr Nazeer's shirt factory, where Amma works. Mr Nazeer lets them live there, very cheap. It is an old caravan with cracks in the walls and concrete blocks instead of wheels. Mrs Kemal and Roshana worked hard to clean it out. People helped with furniture and things.

'What are you doing?' says Roshana's mother, tying up the curtain. 'Here, is this your book? Have you got your sandals on? It's time you were going.'

She gives Jino to Roshana while she takes the pushchair outside and unfolds it. Roshana stands in the doorway, showing her baby brother the feather. He coos and tries to grab it.

'You must pick him up today too,' her mother tells her.

'Are you seeing Rajah, then?' asks Roshana as she puts Jino into his pushchair. Rajah is Amma's new boyfriend. He is younger than Appa was, and very fat.

Mrs Kemal kisses Jino, then Roshana. 'Yes, sweetheart.' She is happy, that's easy to tell. She waves to them as she hurries across the yard to the factory. Jino sucks his fingers and makes a bubbly noise.

Rajah Chowdry works in an office in Gabon Street, upstairs above the shop that sells cooking pots and spices. One day Amma took Roshana and Jino there. It was a tiny room, hot, the air thick with cigarette smoke. Rajah sat squashed behind a desk, smoking, and talking on the phone. He gave her a slice of pineapple, and pinched her cheek. Then he sat Jino on his desk and let him play with the phone.

Rajah wears bright shiny suits and puts greasy pomade on his hair. Whenever Roshana thinks of Rajah, she can smell its powerful sweet smell.

She puts her feather in her pocket. With her satchel on her shoulder and Jino in the pushchair, Roshana sets off for Remya's house.

In town, the streets are busy with people and cars. The sun glares off the white walls and the dusty windows.

Roshana wasn't born here. Nor were her amma and appa. Appa came from the west coast, and Amma from a big plantation, a thousand kilometres away. Roshana has lived in a dozen places in her life, wherever Appa could find work.

That's all changed now.

The flies buzz around in circles. Sometimes Roshana wonders where they think they are going. Jino sings happily to himself, batting at the flies with his hand.

Jino's pushchair is much older than he is. One of the women at the factory had given it to them, and it hadn't been new when she'd had it. The wheels have always squeaked, and now the tyres are worn down to a sliver.

Remya is the old lady who looks after Jino while Amma

is at work. Her house is always full of women and children. Remya answers the door with a baby in one arm and a naked little boy clinging to her sari. She takes Jino easily in her other arm.

'I'll come for him after school,' Roshana tells her.

Remya smiles a toothless smile and blesses Roshana and her mother.

In the crowd waiting to cross Constitution Road, Roshana sees Parvati Ganeri. Parvati clutches her arm. 'Have you done the homework, Roshi?'

'I've done *some* of it . . .'

Parvati rolls her eyes. 'Sister Charity will be cross with you!'

Roshana looks around, squinting against the sunshine. She twists her plait back and forth in her hand. 'Where's Jeeva?'

Jeevamani Anjumbandare is their other friend. Her mother works with Mrs Kemal at the shirt factory. It was Jeeva's mother who had given them the pushchair for Jino, after all her children had grown out of it.

Parvati gives a disapproving sigh. 'Jeeva will be late,' she says. 'As usual!'

Parvati is right. Class has already begun when Jeeva-mani Anjumbandare comes running in. Her hair is coming unplaited, her satchel is undone too. 'Sorry, Sister!' gasps Jeevamani.

Sister Immaculata gives Jeevamani a sorrowful look. Sister Immaculata is one of the nice teachers, gentle and forgiving, generally. When she wants to punish you, she does it with a look. Sister Immaculata looks at you as though your sin would make the angels weep. That's the sort of thing Sister Immaculata is always saying. She holds up her hands and shows her teeth, which are rather long and yellow. 'For shame!' says Sister Immaculata. 'It would make the angels weep!'

The day drags by. The classroom is hot and dark. Through the small barred windows the bright day blazes. Sounds drift in from the world outside: men arguing; dogs barking; traffic going by. Roshana stares at her book, unseeing. She daydreams.

Up ahead at the place where the road forks, the man is standing. He is wearing a turban, a turban so big and round his face is hidden in its shadow.

He is waiting for her.

'Roshana Kemal?'

Roshana jerks awake. Sister Charity is teaching them now. She has obviously asked Roshana a question. Roshana has no idea what it was. 'One hundred,' she says at random. 'One hundred and forty-four.'

Along the bench, Jeevamani cackles and slaps her hand over her mouth. Everyone is sniggering. 'Stupid girl,' says Sister Charity. 'The population of Australia? Anyone else?'

Around the room, all the hands go up.

That evening, when Amma comes home, Jino is asleep in his cot. Roshana is in bed, reading her book. Amma comes to sit with her a little while, as usual. She is excited, full of some momentous news.

'Put that book down, Roshi,' she says. 'I have something to tell you. Something important. Something wonderful!' Her eyes are large and shining.

'Rajah has asked me to marry him,' she says.

Roshana is frightened. She thinks of Rajah. She can smell his pomade.

Her hand smooths the sheet over her knees. She feels a little shy. 'What did you say, Amma?'

Amma glows with pride. 'I told him yes.'

Roshana thinks about a cigarette lying in an ashtray. Smoke curls up from it, blue and bitter.

Amma is frowning at her, frowning and smiling with impatience. 'Well? Roshana? What do you think?'

Roshana doesn't know what she thinks.

'You must be happy, sweetheart,' her mother admonishes her.

'I am, Amma,' says Roshana. 'I'm thinking.'

Amma laughs. 'Don't think too hard,' she says. 'You'll hurt your head.'

Roshana puts a bookmark in her book and sets it aside. She curls up to sleep, but sleep suddenly seems a long way away. She lies and listens to the sounds of Amma on the other side of the curtain, getting ready for bed.

Appa had not been a businessman, like Rajah. Appa was poor. He came from a little fishing village. The gods were unkind, the fishing had been bad, so there was no work for him. He had left home when he was just a boy, and gone travelling from town to town, from job to job, from farm to warehouse to timber yard to building site.

'Amma?' says Roshana.

'What is it, precious?'

Roshana looks at the deep blue evening sky through the window above her bed.

'We can still live here, Amma, can't we?'

She hears her mother laugh. 'Of course not, my sweet! We'll go to live in Rajah's house. All of us together. Won't you like that?'

Roshana doesn't know what she'll like. She wishes Appa were still here to advise her. But of course if Appa were here, Amma would not be talking about marrying Rajah.

Amma leans in at the curtain. She kneels down to speak seriously to her daughter.

'I told Rajah you would be happy for us, Roshi. I told him you would be glad to have a proper father again,' she says gently, almost embarrassedly, 'and live in a nice house.'

She strokes Roshana's cheek. 'Rajah is lucky, Roshi. He was not at all highborn, but he has worked hard and become a wealthy man. He is a good man too, a kind man. This is great good fortune for us, a gift from the gods. We must not say no to good fortune when it comes. Isn't that right, my sweet?'

Roshana reaches up and puts her arms around her mother. She buries her face in her soft body. She tries to nod her head. Of course it's right. It must be.

Chapter 3

Roshana dreams she is standing beneath a tree.

The tree is huge. It goes fifty metres, a hundred metres up into the air. Its trunk is twisted and immense.

Roshana tries to trace the branches of the tree from where they begin, all the way along to where they divide and subdivide. She sees how at first they shoot up into the air, then bow down at the end, all the way down to the ground.

Some of the branches have thrust themselves right into the ground. The buried twigs have turned into roots, and new trunks have sprung up from them. From one tree have grown many others, more than Roshana can count.

She recognizes this great tree then. It is the banyan tree that grows in the meadows by the river. She can see the mist that hangs in its branches.

Roshana is afraid. Everyone knows that where they spring up, the new trunks of a banyan bring ghosts and goblins with them out of the Underworld. She can't see them, but she knows they are there, hiding among the branches. She can almost hear their voices, squeaking, twittering.

Somehow, without quite knowing how, Roshana

seems to have climbed up in the tree. She is balancing on a branch that's as wide as a street, peering among boughs that twist away in all directions out of sight.

It comes to Roshana then that this tree is connected to all the other trees there are. Its roots go down to the centre of the earth, and its branches reach up into heaven. The clouds that hang in its branches are not mist, but clouds of stars.

Chapter 4

Mrs Kemal has given up her job at Mr Nazeer's factory. The family have moved out of the old caravan into Rajah's house on Kosala Road.

Rajah's house is white with a green tile roof. There are palm trees all round it for shade. Rajah has a television and a cocktail cabinet full of different coloured drinks in bottles. In the living room where a fan of brass with wooden blades turns slowly on the ceiling, cooling the air, he keeps an elaborate shrine to Ganesh, the elephant-headed god, whom Roshana thinks he rather resembles.

Rajah loves Jino. He likes to pick him up under the armpits and throw him up in the air. Jino adores this treatment. He squeals with delight, wanting more.

Amma laughs. 'No more,' she cries. 'He'll be sick!'

Rajah takes no notice. He tosses Jino onto the settee, where he lies waving his arms and legs in the air. Rajah tickles him. He pretends to punch him. Jino thinks this is the best fun ever.

Rajah smiles at Roshana and ruffles her hair. 'What did you learn in school?'

'The blue whale, *Balaenoptera musculus*, is the largest living mammal,' recites Roshana. 'It grows up to lengths of thirty metres, and weighs over one hundred and fifty tonnes.'

'Such things they teach nowadays!' Amma exclaims.

Rajah nods approvingly, murmuring something indistinct in a high-pitched voice. He strokes his big belly, smiling uneasily, sweating.

At the wedding Roshana wore a new outfit of tangerine and gold, and carried a basket of flowers. There was a small crowd, mostly people she didn't know. The shrine seemed to be full of fat men in coloured suits and fat women in brilliant saris, all smiling and giggling. Amma was almost unrecognizable in her garlands and gold jewellery. There was a golden medallion on her forehead, and a golden ring through her nose.

The priest took the end of Amma's sari in one hand and the end of Rajah's white scarf in the other, and tied them together in a big knot. Then they had to walk round and round the fire, seven times round in all, while Rajah made his promises in a loud voice. He would keep Amma happy and be faithful to her. He would share his possessions with her, and respect her family. Roshana ground her teeth and looked away. She didn't want his respect. They had been all right as they were, thank you very much.

Jino too was in a bad mood. The heat in the temple and all the strange people made him cross and miserable, and he started to cry. His new aunts crowded round, cooing and clucking their tongues; but Roshana asserted her right to take charge of her brother and carried him outside.

The day was hot. The sky was full of heavy grey clouds, the street was full of traffic. A cow ambled past, accompanied by a skinny man in a loincloth. The cow and the man ignored the squalling baby.

Secretly, Roshana was grateful to Jino for giving her an

excuse to leave the temple. She approved wholeheartedly of his noisy protest. He knew, she thought. Jino knew it was wicked of Amma to take off the white clothes of widowhood and marry again so soon. It was enough to make you suppose she hadn't really loved Appa at all.

The flies settled on Jino's cheeks and forehead. Roshana tried to brush them away. Jino cried louder and kicked as if he thought his big sister was doing him a terrible injury.

'We'll go for a walk,' she told him. 'How will that be?'

She held him firmly to her shoulder and carried him along the street.

Paint flaked from the walls of the buildings. A beggar saw Roshana coming and started to shout. He tried to show her his leg, which was misshapen and wrapped in filthy bandages. Roshana walked on.

Passers-by smiled at her and her wailing baby brother. Their smiles made Roshana cross. She was embarrassed by the attention the pair of them were attracting, she with her festival clothes and Jino with his noise. She gave him a shake.

'Shut up, now, please,' she said. 'Jino. Enough. Be good now.'

Jino smelled bad. He waved his arms and bellowed.

They passed a confectionery stand, and then the loading bay of a warehouse. The door was open, the steel shutter rolled up. In the cavernous dark interior an ancient lorry stood shuddering, ready to come rumbling out into the street. The noise of the lorry made Jino still more angry and unhappy.

The high wall of the warehouse was covered in posters advertising movies. Men clutching women in dancers' costumes stood pointing guns at each other. The women were stretching their eyes wide and pouting. Roshana hurried on.

At the corner there was a man in a long, brightly patterned skirt and a very large, very white turban. He stood against the wall with his arms folded. His head was turned towards Roshana and Jino.

Jino gave a hiccough and fell silent.

The man looked for all the world as if he was standing there waiting for them. Roshana didn't recognize him. For some reason the sight of him made her nervous.

Roshana stopped. She stood hesitating, jiggling her little brother in her arms. He was quiet – eerily so, considering how much noise he'd been making two seconds before.

Roshana decided it was time to start back for the temple.

The lorry was still inside the warehouse, its engine making spluttering noises, filling the loading bay with smoke. Roshana ran in front of it. She hurried past the red and yellow stand. There was a young woman there now, buying a portion of coconut ice.

The young woman noticed Roshana coming and started to wave and shout.

'Roshana! Roshana Kemal!'

It was Smita Anjumbandare, Jeeva's big sister.

'Look at you, look at you! So beautiful! Where are you rushing off to in those lovely clothes?'

Smita was dressed up, as always, and wearing heaps of make-up. Smita is not very tall, but she wears her hair combed up very high on top of her head, and she gets high heels from the shoe shop where she works. She looks just like one of the poster women, Roshana thinks.

'Oh my goodness!' cried Smita. 'Of course, the wedding! Your mother's wonderful wedding, how absolutely scrumptious!'

That's the way Smita talks all the time, at the top of her voice, with a maximum of exclamation and fuss. She sounded now as if the mere fact of a wedding going on somewhere was enough to make her explode with agitation. Smita is eighteen, though she looks all of twenty-five.

'It's nearly over,' said Roshana automatically. 'They are all going back to the house. You must come, Smita, why don't you?'

Roshana did not actually want Smita Anjumbandare to come to the wedding celebrations. She had mentioned the house because Smita had once come to the caravan with her mother. She had refused to come inside. 'The caravan is too small for everyone!' she'd said frantically. She had stood in Mr Nazeer's yard, smiling and bobbing her head, and wiping her hands together, over and over, as if she was afraid she might have touched something dirty.

Roshana wanted Smita Anjumbandare to know that her family has a house now, a proper one.

Smita was blinking rapidly. She was wearing false eyelashes, very black and very long. Sometimes at break Jeevamani does imitations of her sister in front of the mirror, putting her eyelashes on, and makes them all scream with laughter.

'Oh! I should love to come to the house! I should love to, more than anything else in the universe!' cried Smita. 'Here, here, Roshana darling, have some coconut ice.'

She thrust the paper cone at her. Roshana was already shaking her head, but Smita wasn't taking any notice. She probably wasn't even aware that Roshana was refusing,

though she was looking right at her. Smita wore a dazzling smile that took in the sweet vendor, the bandaged
beggar, and half the people on the other side of the street.
'It is the best coconut ice in the universe!'

She gazed adoringly at Jino. Her voice went up very
high.

'And who is this, then? Who is this? Of course! Of
course, my sweet, this is your darling little baby brother!
What a pet! Isn't he the sweetest creature in the universe?'

'This is Jino,' said Roshana, trying her best to pull her
brother back from the frightening face now zooming at
him, without offending its owner, and without toppling
backwards into the traffic.

Jino just stared at Smita, too startled to utter a sound.

Smita said that Jino was a heavenly name, and Jino was
a heavenly baby. She was sure he would like some coconut ice. His sister said yes, she was sure he would, when
he got some teeth.

'I should like to have a hundred babies,' Smita told the
world in general, offering Roshana her cone again and
ignoring her refusal again. 'Oh, I wish they could possibly
be a hundredth as sweet as yours!' She almost seemed to
have the impression that Roshana was Jino's mother, not
his sister.

Roshana walked away, quickly, before Smita could
form the idea of coming with them. She could hear her
as they went, calling down blessings on her mother and
Rajah, and on all the babies in the universe. She hoped
Smita didn't know their new address. She was quite
capable of turning up, unaccompanied, unannounced.

At the temple, the wedding party was coming out.
People were cheering, applauding, taking photographs.

Roshana saw Aunt Lifafa, Amma's sister, who had taken two days to make the journey here with her husband and children. Aunt Lifafa swooped down on Roshana and whisked Jino away. 'Your basket!' hissed Aunt Lifafa. 'Quick, Roshi, quick!'

Roshana grabbed her basket of flower petals just in time. All the guests, known and unknown, jostled her as they dug handfuls out of it to fling over the heads of the bride and groom, who were laughing and scrambling into the special white car Rajah had hired.

Back at the house, the celebrations had begun. Ganesh's shrine was heaped so high with flowers and fruit that you could hardly see him. The air was a cloud of sandalwood and jasmine, loud with music and merriment.

Roshana pushed through the crowd until she found her mother. Amma embraced her in a crushing cloud of silk and perfume, glass bangles and garlands and jewels. The palms of her hands were decorated with patterns of lacy red paint. 'Thank you, darling, you are an angel. Isn't she, Rajah?'

Her stepfather seized Roshana and kissed her. 'She is a treasure!' he proclaimed. 'Our little nursemaid!'

For a moment, the scent of his pomade overcame the incense. Then he released Roshana and made a grab for Jino. He circled the room holding Jino above his head, spreadeagled in the air. Jino squealed and kicked, his earlier bad temper quite forgotten.

All the guests laughed and cheered. Roshana was pushed back against the wall next to the buffet table. She watched Rajah showing off with her baby brother. When she caught his eye he looked away immediately. He hated her, she knew he did. It was Jino he loved, though only as long as he could play with him like a toy. And Amma, now, only had eyes for Rajah.

Roshana picked at a plate of jellabies. Life was very hard, and very long. Her stepfather's big house, with its electric refrigerator and circling fan and flushing toilet, was truly only a prison. She wondered how many years she would have to live there before she could escape.

Chapter 5

The birds won't stay in the sky. There are a lot of them, a whole mob of great big black birds, all falling out of the sky. They keep dropping straight down, like bombs, as if they're trying on purpose to fall on you.

They're a nuisance. They're ugly. Their plumage is hard and shiny; more like steel than feathers. There's one in particular that seems to have its eye on Roshana. She's running to get out of the way. She's running through the streets, but the streets all lead to wide open places with nowhere to shelter.

Now she sees a wall ahead with some trees on the other side. It looks as if there may be a park there, or a garden. Roshana hurries to the wall and scrambles over it. She runs to a tree.

When she gets behind it, she realizes there is someone else there already, sheltering from the birds. She looks around and sees that all the trees have people behind them, hiding.

Now, someone offers to take her to a house. She follows them. They go down into the ground. The house is down there, hidden, a secret. It's a big house, with many rooms and passages. Many people live there. Roshana goes from room to room, seeing them, seeing what they're doing: cooking, talking, washing, sleeping. She has someone with her now, someone small. It's Jino. Of course it is. She has to protect him too.

She goes into the next room and sees that though it is underground, it has a window. Through the window she can see the grass of the park and the big ugly birds, mobbing to and fro. She feels a great sadness and frustration that she and Jino are still not safe. Even down here there is a place where the birds can get in.

The man who's showing them around doesn't seem to understand the problem. He tries to reassure her, to tell her everything's all right. He points to a table, spread with a dazzling white cloth. On the table is a white plate. On the plate is a slice of pineapple.

Roshana turns away.

In the grass outside the window, she can see something running about. It looks like some kind of animal. She can see its furry back. It's yellow with spots on. She can see its pointed ears. It's a dog. The dog is grinning, coming for Roshana, and she wakes, sitting bolt upright in bed.

The night is hot and sticky. The insects are whining.

Roshana has no idea what has frightened her. She must have been having a dream. She lies down again on her pillow.

Here in Rajah's house, for the first time in her life Roshana has her own bedroom. It's a wonderful luxury. She has her own dressing table and chair.

It is a bit lonely, though, having your own room. When she was little, if ever she woke up in the night with a scary dream, Amma and Appa would be there to cuddle her until she went back to sleep.

She can't call out to Amma now, because Rajah would

hear her. It would be worse than anything, to let Rajah
know that she is unhappy or afraid.

She lies on her back staring up into the dark. Her heart
is pounding as if she had just run home from somewhere a
long way away.

Chapter 6

Rajah has a car, a big one from America. It is a 1995 Chrysler, he tells everyone. It has independent suspension and air conditioning.

Rajah is proud of his car. He sits in the driving seat with the steering wheel pressing into his stomach, and drives his new family up into the hills.

It's a long journey. Amma sits in the back with Jino on her lap. He babbles for a while, excited at being in the car; then he grows tired and starts to cry. Amma tries to soothe him.

Roshana sits in the front, next to Rajah. The air conditioning whirrs, filling the car with the mingled smells of her stepfather's pomade and the cigarettes he smokes. That and the motion, the bends and bumps in the road combine to make Roshana feel slightly sick.

Behind her, Amma is singing a lullaby to Jino. Roshana turns round to look at them but it's not comfortable, sitting twisted round like that. She faces the front again, the dry rutted road jolting towards them. She sings Amma's lullaby to herself, inside her head. She doesn't sing it out loud. Roshana doesn't feel like singing aloud with Rajah sitting beside her. His bulk silences her as completely as if he were sitting on top of her.

'Look at those greedy birds!' says Amma, in a scolding voice. Roshana looks. They are passing terraced fields, plants standing in line, row upon row, tier upon tier. The plants go by like waves of leaves. The leaves are dull green and dusty for lack of rain. Big birds hop among them, pecking them rapidly and determinedly. Children run around with sticks, to scare the birds away. Roshana sees the birds fly up, slowly, lazily, as though they have no fear of the children but do it anyway, out of habit. They circle and settle again, in another field.

Villages appear and disappear. They have been driving for hours. Roshana doesn't actually know where they are going. No one has bothered to tell her, and she will not ask.

All she knows is that all week Amma has been baking, making sweets and biscuits and putting them in tins. Before they left, Amma had her carry the tins out to the car and put them in the boot.

It used to be that Amma talked to her all the time, discussing everything with her. Nothing would ever happen without Roshana knowing about it.

Now it is Rajah that Amma tells everything to. They shut themselves up together in their room. Roshana knows they are happy, that they love one another and want to be alone together, but it makes her feel lonely and left out. She wants Amma to understand but if she doesn't, she can't tell her. She rubs the window of the car with her finger.

The road gets worse. The wheels spin and kick up stones. The engine whines. Rajah battles with the steering wheel, blowing between his teeth. The car lurches as the road climbs up among high rocks. Goats stare down at them, looking witless and half-starved.

They come to another village. This one is built into the hillside. The houses are made of whitewashed stone. They all look scuffed and stained. Flights of stone steps lead up to crooked wooden verandahs. The verandahs have been painted in bright colours, but not recently. There are old women sitting on them, peeling piles of vegetables, mending clothes. Below, children play in the dirt. The smallest of them are naked. The children all stare at the approaching car, as if it were something marvellous to see.

Rajah pulls up outside one of the houses. Roshana sees window shutters patched with pieces of cardboard and corrugated iron; a rusty wringer on the verandah. She looks round. Amma is smiling.

Some of the bolder children have followed them. When they start to get out of the car the children hang back warily. Roshana notices at once that it is much cooler up here than it was back in town.

Rajah is waving to the children. 'Hello, Manjula! Sumi! Rekha!'

They don't seem to recognize him. They whisper to-gether. They run to the car, keeping low, as if expecting missiles. They climb up and look in the back window.

Amma seems nervous. She holds Jino propped on her hip in one arm while she fusses with her tins and bags. 'Roshi, there's a good girl, help me here now . . .' Jino is still asleep, his head and one arm flopping backwards like a doll. Roshana takes him from her mother. She holds him close, his head on her shoulder.

From somewhere inside the house a dog appears. It stands at the top of the steps, barking wildly.

That makes Roshana anxious. A big dog knocked her over once, when she was just a little girl, hardly more than a baby. She can almost remember it: the huge hairy shadow lunging at her without warning, out of the sun. And then the pain of grazed skin, down both her shins, on the palms of her hands where she had flung them out in front of her instinctively as she fell. Amma had made a great fuss, and Appa too. He had grabbed a stick and threatened to hit the dog, and its owner too, while Roshana wept with pain and shock. She has been frightened of dogs ever since.

This dog is a scrawny black mongrel bitch with matted fur. It races down the steps and jumps up at Rajah, barking loud enough to wake Jino, who blinks and screws up his face. He rubs his fist sleepily in his eyes.

Rajah goes down on one knee, petting the horrible dog, making a fuss of her. 'There's a good girl, Nula. Good girl! Yes, I'm happy to see you too.'

Amma is heading for the steps. Roshana follows her, walking carefully round behind the dog, avoiding its flailing tail.

At the top of the steps now there is an old woman leaning on a walking stick. She has white hair and a face with deep creases in it. She wears a pink sari, grubby, thin and faded, with the end up over her head. Her arms are as thin as Jino's.

Rajah calls out to her in a language Roshana doesn't know. She understands that the old woman is Rajah's mother.

The black dog barks and barks, dashing backwards and forwards around Rajah, butting him with its head. Amma is at the bottom of the steps, calling Roshana forward, trying to pull something out of one of her bags. It is a tin.

Amma takes Jino from Roshana and puts the tin in her hands. 'Here, Roshi, give this to Mrs Chowdry.'

Roshana carries the tin up the steps. She feels as if they might fall apart beneath her. She will fall through and be dashed to pieces on the rocky ground. Behind her, Jino starts to cry.

The eyes of the old woman are as white as pebbles washed by the river. She seems pleased to see Roshana. She pats her on the shoulder and says something to her. Her voice sounds like a crow.

Roshana looks over her shoulder. The others are coming up the steps now. Amma is grinning madly, gesturing to her to give the old woman the tin.

Roshana gives it to her and watches her open it. Her hands are crazed and wrinkled as ancient leather. The tin is full of jellabies. The old woman smiles and croaks and nods. She steers Roshana into the house.

Inside, it is cool and dark. An old man, as old and as wrinkly as the old woman, comes shuffling forward to greet them. He embraces Rajah, patting him on the back and grinning with a mouth entirely empty of teeth. Rajah presents Amma to him and he embraces her too, enjoying it. The smell of him is terrible, sour and unclean.

Other people appear, six, seven, a dozen of them. Rajah hands round cigarettes. The children come running in. They stare at Roshana, at her clothes. Roshana feels lost and shy. She cannot speak, only nod and smile.

They sit in fraying basket chairs and drink milky tea and eat sweetmeats. Roshana is glad then that the sweetmeats are her mother's, and out of her mother's tins. She would not like to eat anything made in this dirty, smelly house.

Jino is too young to care. He sits on the old woman's knee and sucks flakes of honeycake from her finger. He chokes, then sneezes, and laughs in surprise at himself, a gurgling baby laugh. Everybody laughs. Everybody is happy, except Roshana. They are talking about her now. Amma puts her hand on Roshana's head. 'She is a bit of a dreamer, this one!' she announces. 'She is a good girl, though, and very helpful when she puts her mind to it. She takes great care of Jino.'

Rajah translates everything back and forth, beaming as if Roshana and Jino were his own children and he himself responsible for all their evident virtues.

Roshana thinks about her real father's family. She wonders what life is like where they live, by the sea. She desperately wants to be there.

After Appa's accident, Amma wrote to tell his parents, and they wrote back, begging them to come. They would have found room to take them in, Roshana and Amma and the unborn baby; but Amma would not let them go. They should stay where they had friends, she'd said; and there was work at the factory. Roshana understands that Appa's parents might well have found Amma a new husband too, among their other sons.

Still, Roshana wishes Amma had not said no. She wishes they had gone to live there, in a shack by the ocean. She would have learned to sail one of the painted wooden boats. She imagines dipping the tarry black nets into the shining water and pulling up a catch of bright fish, slippery and silver.

Dogs trot in and out of the horrid, shabby house. The black one, Nula, keeps sniffing around Roshana's feet. She seems to know the girl is afraid of her.

'You're not afraid of the dog, Roshi, are you?' says Amma. 'A big girl like you.' She laughs at her, excusing her daughter's poor manners to the old couple. Darkness seems to crowd into Roshana's head from all around. She is ashamed, and miserable. Amma is laughing at her, betraying her.

Roshana is sure the dog is laughing at her too.

Chapter 7

It's late at night when the family get back from the village in the hills. When the car pulls up outside the house on Kosala Road, Jino and Roshana have been asleep for some time. Roshana is dreaming about a road that runs through tall green grass. Sometimes it is a road, sometimes more like a river. It carries her along swiftly, without her having to move her feet. Roshana does not even know if she wants to go where the river-road is taking her.

The car stopping wakes her. She sees Rajah's round face smiling above her like a dark moon. 'Safe home,' says Rajah.

Roshana sulks. This house would never be *her* home, whatever he said.

Amma carries the sleeping Jino between the palm trees to the gate. 'Come along, Roshi,' she says. 'I know you're tired, but be a good girl now. Help your father with the bags.'

As soon as everyone and everything is safe indoors and the doors shut, Roshana gives Rajah a dutiful kiss, her mother a more affectionate one, and Jino a tiny one on the top of the head, a kiss as light as a feather falling, so as

not to wake him. Then she hauls herself by the polished
wooden banister, upstairs to bed.

In bed, Roshana has another dream. She dreams she is
still up, and walking through the house. The dream is so
vivid she thinks she is awake. The electric lights gleam on
the polished wood, and on the brass bowl that stands on
the windowsill, on the landing. A breeze creeps under the
door and up the stairs. The flowered curtains stir.

Rajah's house has two floors, yet in the dream the stairs
go on up to a third floor, and a fourth. Roshana is not
surprised by this. It seems as if she always knew the other
floors were there, but had not got around to exploring
them. She walks along hallways of closed doors, all
painted white. No lights shine under the doors. The
rooms within must be in darkness.

Beside Roshana walks an animal. It has short yellow fur
with spots on, and big pointed ears. Its tail is heavy and
bushy. Roshana doesn't remember the other dream she
had, about the house under the ground. She doesn't
realize this is the same animal she caught sight of then,
running through the grass outside the window. She
thinks again that it must be a dog, but for some reason
she is not afraid of it. Nor does she think it strange, in the
dream, when the animal speaks to her.

Sivalu, it says. *That's my name. Remember me, Roshana?*
Sivalu.

Sivalu pushes his long white nose against one of the
closed white doors. He lifts one of his forefeet and paws at
it, just like a dog.

Roshana reaches for the handle of the door. She cannot
feel it, in the dream, but she turns it and the door opens.

Inside, there is a man in a brightly coloured *lungi* and a
big white turban with a black feather stuck in it. He is

watching television. Roshana thinks he seems familiar, but she can't see who he is because his face is turned away.

It is not Roshana's room, and she knows she shouldn't, but she goes in anyway. She wants to see the man.

She goes up to him and sees that he is old. He is the oldest person she has ever seen.

His face is dark, darker even than her own. His skin is crazed and wrinkled. His eyes are like holes in leather. He looks like an ancient leather waterbottle with a face. He sits holding his hand across his face in an odd way, pressing the tip of his middle finger and thumb to either cheek.

He is wearing a mask, a smiling mask. He is holding it to his face. As Roshana sees that, the mask slips slightly.

She wakes then, gasping, short of breath. The heat of the night lies upon her like a blanket. The white curtains hang lifeless at her window.

She remembers the dream, bits of it, all muddled up. Sivalu was in it. Roshana remembers Sivalu. He was in a story Amma used to tell her when she was a little girl.

Sivalu was a jackal, a clever jackal that belonged to Jamil the weaver. Jamil loved the princess in the palace. With his cleverness, Sivalu made the princess so impressed with his master that she fell in love with him. They got married, Jamil and the princess, and lived happily ever after.

Roshana hasn't thought of Sivalu for years. She wonders what he was doing in her dream. Plumping up her pillow and turning over in bed, she thinks about the man who was in it too, the man who was holding a mask to his face. When the mask slipped, she saw beneath it the face of her stepfather, Rajah.

Chapter 8

'They're so poor. And so dirty,' Roshana tells her friends at morning break. 'The kids all had snot running out of their noses.'

'Ugh!' says Jeevamani, pulling a face.

'And Rajah's father *stinks*!'

'*Ugh*!' say Jeevamani and Parvati together.

'He has never had a bath in his life.' Roshana states this for a fact, though actually she is making it up. She doesn't really know anything about the old man in the mountain village, or his family. Nor does she want to, thank you very much.

Parvati seems to care more about Rajah's relations than Roshana does. Parvati Ganeri cares about everyone and everything. 'It's so awful, Roshi,' she says, waving away a fly. 'Those poor people.'

The girls are under the jacaranda tree that grows behind the school. It is their special place, for seniors only. They lounge in the shade watching the juniors skipping in the sun. Roshana and Jeevamani are sitting on the ground. Parvati is standing with her back to the trunk, her head tipped back.

'If Rajah has so much money, why doesn't he bring them to live here?' says Jeevamani.

Roshana makes a face. 'Because he's a greedy, selfish man.' Jeevamani agrees vehemently, loyally.

In fact, Rajah had given his father money. Roshana had seen him put some in his hands, before they left to come home. Goodness knows, they needed it. The place was like a rubbish dump.

Parvati embraces the jacaranda tree backwards, hugging it between her elbows. The sunlight falls through the leaves and speckles her face. 'They could live in his house.'

'No thank you!' cries Roshana.

'No, Roshi, listen!' says Jeevamani. 'If they came to live there, maybe you could go home.' She speaks excitedly, tugging at the fat black plait of her hair. At this moment she clearly believes her idea is a sensible one, something that could actually happen.

Roshana says nothing. The caravan in the factory yard suddenly seems a long time ago. Other people are living there now, Amma says, relatives of another of Mr Nazeer's workers.

'Smita wants to marry Arun and move to the city,' says Jeevamani. Her mind is renowned for the ease with which it jumps from improbability to improbability. Grasshopper, Sister Immaculata calls her.

Roshana and Parvati know about Jeevamani's big sister Smita and her secret boyfriend. Jeeva has told them about him more than once.

Arun is some years older than Smita. He lives in the city, and works on one of the big ferryboats that go across the river. First, Jeeva had said he was a pilot, but then she forgot she'd told them that and admitted he was only a deckhand, one of the men who get the cars and the livestock on and off the boat.

Mr and Mrs Anjumbandare must never hear about Arun. They would not approve of their daughter consorting with a man at all, let alone one they don't know. In any case, Arun's caste is too low. You are not supposed to say that now, or even think it, but everyone does. It is like Roshana's mother and Rajah Chowdry.

'Smita says if Arun doesn't ask her to marry him she will die!' Jeevamani falls on her back in the grass, hugging herself ecstatically.

'She hardly knows him,' objects Roshana.

Jeevamani defends her sister. 'She sees him every time she goes to see the cousins.'

It's important to visit your relatives, everyone knows, but there are quite a lot of Anjumbandares and though they have pride, they have little money. The Anjumbandare cousins who live in the city have rather more money than Jeevamani's parents, or so Roshana understands. In any case, the Anjumbandares are very particular about visiting the city cousins, on feast days and birthdays. At Diwali the whole family goes, and the rest of the year they send a representative to take presents and pay the family's respects. It used to be Jeeva's big brother who went, but now he is in the army and the duty has fallen to Smita. She goes on the train with a neighbour of theirs, an old man who used to live in the city himself.

'Mr Masulkur thinks she's with the cousins, but Smita slips away!'

Parvati sighs. 'You can't put a fence round love,' she says. It is an old proverb but she says it with conviction, as if Smita's behaviour proves the truth of it.

The juniors shout and shriek in the sunshine. Under the

jacaranda tree, the three friends fall silent. They wonder what it must be like, to be in love with someone. They all have their own ideas. Parvati's are romantic and serious; Jeevamani's, exciting and confusing. Roshana is the least enthusiastic. She is aware that she is living in the house of love, and she does not like it. It makes her uncomfortable, as if someone had taken away her favourite chair and left nowhere for her to sit down.

Sister Martha blows her whistle, putting an end to games and dreams. The girls troop back inside to learn about viruses and alluvial valleys.

That Sunday, Roshana sits alone at the dining table, doing her homework. She has to read a story in English, about an Englishwoman shopping in a vast department store, and then answer questions about it. She wonders why English is such a complicated language, all exceptions and irregularities. She realizes she has left her Pocket English Dictionary up in her room and she goes up to fetch it.

The house is perfectly silent. Amma is out, visiting a neighbour, and she has taken Jino with her. Where Rajah has got to, Roshana has no idea.

The sunlight shines through the flowered curtains at the window on the landing and gleams on the brass bowl that stands on the sill. The way the curtains stir as she passes reminds Roshana of something, but she can't remember what. She goes along the hallway to her room, passing Amma and Rajah's room on the way. The door is open. Rajah is in there, bending over something on the dressing table.

When Appa was travelling, he used to write letters to Amma. Letters of love, letters about his life and hopes for their future together. Amma still has them all. She keeps

them in a special box, a box of red felt embroidered with
white and yellow flowers, with tiny round mirrors in the
middles of the flowers. Through the door of the bedroom
Roshana sees Amma's box open on the dressing table.
Rajah is reading Appa's letters.

Roshana is incensed. Without thinking she marches
straight in.

'What are you doing, you thief, you spy? Those letters
are my Appa's! They are private, they belong to my
mother! How dare you read them?'

Her stepfather straightens up, staring at her, eyes wide,
mouth open. He looks like a baby caught stealing a biscuit.

Roshana snatches at the letter he holds in his hand. He
holds it away from her, up in the air. He grabs for her
shoulder and pushes her away, trying to keep her at arm's
length.

It makes Roshana even angrier to be defied. She hears
her stepfather shouting at her, telling her not to be stupid,
asking what in the name of all the gods she thinks she is
doing. Roshana shouts back at him, not knowing what
she is saying, what names she is calling him. She snatches
again at the letter and catches hold of a corner of it. He
pulls, she pulls, and the paper tears. The corner comes
away in Roshana's hand.

Roshana suddenly sees and hears her stepfather very
clearly. He seems very large in the sunlit bedroom. He
looms over her like an offended bull.

'Look what you've done, wicked girl! Your mother will
be very unhappy!'

Roshana gasps. 'It's your fault! You shouldn't have
been reading them!'

Rajah grimaces, enraged. Then suddenly he softens. He
pats her on the arm.

'Roshana, Jyoti doesn't mind if I read the letters. She is happy for me to read them. We share them. That's the way we do things in this house, isn't it? We share things. This bed. This is mine. I share it with your mother. This roof, these walls. All mine, in fact. Aren't they?'

Roshana keeps her mouth shut. He is speaking quietly now, and being very patient.

'We share them all together. That's the way it is, Roshi. Roshi, look at me. Aren't you happy here?'

'No!' Roshana is angry. Her face is rigid.

Rajah is not disturbed. 'Your mother and I hope you will learn,' he says. 'We want you to be happy, Roshi. You have everything you want. Isn't that right? If you want something, anything, you have only to ask me.'

'I want you to leave Appa's letters alone,' says Roshana. As she says it, her courage evaporates, and she hears her voice go all miserable and whiny, like a little girl's. Tears start into her eyes.

Roshana will not let this tyrant with his vast trousers and his solid gold rings make her cry. She looks down, biting back the tears. There is the corner of Appa's letter in her fingers. It has little curly ink marks on it, the torn remains of words, like dead insects.

Rajah puts his hands on her arms. 'I love your father. I honour him, and cherish his memory.'

Gently he takes the little triangle of paper from her. He holds it against the torn edge of the sheet it came from. When he holds it with his great thumb across the tear, the sheet looks whole.

'These letters, Roshi. They are not your Appa.'

He lays the two pieces of the sheet carefully together on the dressing table.

'He is dead, my sweet. He is dead. And now it is today.'

He has gone down on one knee to embrace her.

'I am your Appa now.'

He holds her delicately, as if she might snap in two. Stiffly, Roshana lets him press his huge soft cheek to hers. She doesn't know what to think. What he is saying is true, she knows that. She is protected and well fed. Yet she cannot accept that a man she hardly knows and doesn't like is allowed to rummage through Amma's belongings, when Amma is not there. Why did Amma choose him? They were all right as they were, the three of them, Amma and Roshana and Jino.

Perhaps she is being stupid, and wicked. What would the Sisters say? *You must be grateful, Roshana. You must try to be good . . .*

Without a word Roshana goes away into her room and shuts the door. She pulls her photo off the wall, the one of her with Amma and Appa in the meadow. She throws herself on the bed and pulls her knees up tight, clutching her photo to her chest.

Rajah's scent is still in her nostrils. She feels a wave of anger wash back through her, weaker now.

'If Appa were here, he would get rid of you in two seconds!' says Roshana in the direction of the door. But she does not say it loud enough for Rajah to hear.

Chapter 9

That night, Roshana dreams of dogs again, yellow dogs, bigger than she is. There are two of them and they have four eyes each.

The dogs roll their eyes and gnash their great teeth at her. They are barking. The sound of their barking comes faintly to Roshana's ears, as if the dogs were a lot farther away than they seem.

Long, long chains of hard black iron lead from the dogs to the gates of what must be a fortress. The gates tower up into the sky, which is purple and black. They are made of wood so ancient it has turned to coal.

High up on the gates Roshana can see a line of skulls hanging. The skulls gape down at her in despair. They tell her this is Kalichi, the Palace of the End of All Things.

Roshana sees the dogs again. They wear collars set with long yellow spikes. Roshana knows that those spikes are the teeth of other ferocious beasts that the dogs have killed.

Someone sits looking down at her from the back of a water buffalo. She looks and sees that it is a man, or something with the shape of a man.

His robes are red as blood, and his hands are full of weapons.

Roshana knows who he is. He is Yama, the Lord of the Dead, the King of the Underworld. This is how he looks when he comes to claim a soul.

Yama looms over Roshana, snorting like an offended bull. His eyes are made of copper, his face is bright green. He holds up a sheet of paper with one corner torn off. Roshana can see writing on the paper, her father's writing. As she watches, the paper starts to burn.

'He's not my Appa,' she tells the green man. 'This is my Appa.'

Appa is there now, with a rope around his neck. Otherwise, he is just as Roshana remembers him: a muscular man with a moustache and a bushy beard. He lifts her up onto his shoulders as if she weighs nothing.

Now she is as tall as Yama on his buffalo, but she is frightened of falling. Yama roars like a bull. He holds the end of Appa's rope in his hand.

Roshana falls. Her eyes hold the image of the black feather in Yama's turban. As she falls his green face turns black, black and old, like the gates of the fortress.

The ancient face winks at Roshana.

Chapter 10

After lunch, Roshana and Parvati sit in the shade of the jacaranda tree, talking about dreams.

'He is always there, always, waiting for me,' says Roshana, exaggerating slightly. She can still see Yama's rolling copper eyes, his face turning black and wrinkled. 'Every time I go to sleep,' she says, 'I dream of him.'

Parvati looks up at her with big eyes.

'Dreams come true, Roshi,' she says. 'They do. I read it in a magazine. There was this one woman who had a dream about finding a diamond in a field of rice. She thought it was just a dream, not worth anything, and then one day she was looking through some of her mother's things, and she found this brooch that her mother had lost ages before, a diamond brooch. And where do you think it was? In a rice pot!'

'He is so *old*, Parvati,' says Roshana. She grimaces and drags her fingers down her cheeks. 'He's like a horrible old black spider waiting to catch me.'

Roshana pulls her dress tight around her knees. She glares resentfully at the juniors playing in the sunshine.

'I'm going to pray for you, Roshi,' says Parvati seriously.

'I'm going to pray to Lord Krishna and Lord Jesus to keep you safe. You must pray too.'

Roshana says nothing. With one hand she grubs in the dirt among the roots of the tree, trying to pull up a little clump of weeds. She is sure the man she keeps dreaming about has something to do with Rajah. He was Rajah, that one time, Rajah in a mask.

She will not mention that to Parvati. She doesn't want to hear what Parvati's interpretation of that would be.

The sun blazes down. The leaves of the tree are parched and shrivelled. It will be some time yet before the rains come.

Jeevamani, who has been kept back by Sister Charity for a test result of nought out of twenty, comes running to them across the playground. She stops and gazes down at her preoccupied friend.

'Roshana, you look so miserable!'

'Leave her alone, Jeeva,' says Parvati protectively. 'Roshi is not feeling well.'

Jeevamani at once looks concerned. She is the most sympathetic soul in all the world. 'What is it, Roshi? Have you got a pain?'

Parvati puts her arm around Roshana, trying to shield her from Jeevamani's impetuous curiosity. 'Roshi is having awful dreams.'

Jeevamani drops to her knees, excited by the prospect of a mystery. 'What do you dream about, Roshi? Is it a terrible *man* coming to get you?'

Parvati rolls up her eyes in exasperation. Roshana looks away.

Jeevamani knows now that she has accidentally hit on the truth or something very near it. She starts stalking about stiff-legged like some hideous movie monster, her hands stretched out in front of her. '*Oo-ooh*, Roshana, the tall dark stranger is coming to carry you off!'

Parvati shouts at her twice, three times, to shut up. Then she starts to snigger.

Roshana returns to pulling weeds. She feels wretched. A horrible man has come and stolen her mother and ruined their home, sleep has become a nightly torment, and all her friends can do is prance about giggling like juniors.

'*Mmm*, Roshana dreams about *men*! Dark handsome men who come to her in her dreams . . .'

Jeevamani shrieks with laughter. She bounces up and down, her fat black pigtail flying.

Sister Immaculata comes striding across the playground, clapping her hands. 'Jeevamani Anjumbandare! For shame!' Her rosary swings wildly at her hip. 'Modesty, young lady, modesty!'

Afternoon school is dull, interminable, all about logarithms and the principle of angular momentum. Roshana almost nods off. She blinks and buries her hands in her pockets, holding her arms stiffly to her sides, trying to stretch without the teacher noticing. In one of the pockets of her pinafore dress her hand finds something prickly.

Surreptitiously, she pulls it out and looks at it.

It is the feather she found beside her bed, on the floor of the old caravan. It was that morning, the morning of the day when Amma told her she was going to get married again and they were going to go and live with Rajah.

The feather is a bit crooked now, a bit battered from being carried around in her pocket. Roshana's not at all sure it hasn't been through the washing machine.

As Sister Martha twitters on about the coefficient of the tangent, Roshana tries to smooth her feather out on her thigh beneath the desk. The little barbs are set in two perfect smooth rows, one either side of the shaft. They are all stuck together, like the teeth of a zip. When you separate them, you can feel the tiny resistance as they peel smoothly away from one another. It's a very satisfying feeling, Roshana thinks, pulling the barbs of the feather mercilessly apart, one by one.

They never go back together though, no matter how hard you try.

Chapter 11

The Shadowman stands in a fork of the banyan tree. Behind him, several branches have become entangled in a fabulous, complicated knot. Roshana sees the smile on the face of the Shadowman and she knows he tied that knot himself, with his bare hands.

His long clothes stir and sway as if in a breeze. The multicoloured patterns on them change, making pictures, like a film on a screen. When she sees that, Roshana understands that she is dreaming again. The dream is as clear and firm as being awake. Knowing it's a dream changes nothing.

The pictures on the Shadowman's clothes show Roshana and her parents on the train with all their belongings, their clothes and cooking pots. They are moving from one place to another, one job to another. Roshana sees Appa on the building site, high up on the scaffolding. She opens her mouth to shout, to warn him, but no sound comes out. She tries to run to him, but her feet will not move. The scaffolding gives way, and once again Roshana's Appa falls.

The Shadowman's clothing stirs. The folds of his *lungi* close and open.

Roshana sees a picture of Rajah's house. She sees herself walking along the hallway of white-painted doors. One of the doors stands open. A black dog guards the threshold, a scrawny mongrel bitch with matted fur. Roshana struggles to go back.

The Shadowman reaches for her hand. *Come to me*, he says. *Don't be afraid. I'll take care of you.*

He holds out a black feather.

Chapter 12

On Saturday, after their chores are done, the girls meet to walk out to the river. Roshana has Jino with her, in his pushchair. Though Amma has given up her job, she still offloads him onto Roshana whenever she can. 'The fresh air will do him good.'

Sometimes Roshana feels no better than an *aya*, a nursemaid.

'I could take him to Remya,' she offered this morning, not for the first time.

Amma said what she always says. 'Too far.' It isn't too far at all, or it wouldn't be if Rajah would take him, in his car.

The truth is, Rajah disapproves of Amma sending her child to an old woman who is poor and shabby, who is not even a relative.

Rajah disapproves. Rajah, who's not a relative either.

Along the river, men sit fishing, relishing the slightest hint of chill. Insects whirr in the shining air.

Roshana is fed up with her mother. All she does these days is drink tea and watch TV. She hasn't got time for Jino, but she always has time to gossip with the neighbours, to swap recipes for wonderful meals to make for big fat Rajah. Amma is getting used to the luxury of leisure.

'Look, Jino! Hummingbird!'

The bird hovers over the path, its little wings beating so fast you can't see them. Jino reaches for it. Parvati and Jeevamani laugh.

Roshana's friends always love to see Jino. They like to play with him, holding him upright, making him kick his legs, practising for the day he will learn to walk. He will get up onto all fours now, all by himself, but he doesn't know what to do when he gets there. Parvati and Jeevamani get down on the floor with him. They tease him with their long hair, tickling him with it, making him laugh and sneeze. When one of them holds him, Jino grabs a handful of her hair and pulls it, making her squeal. 'Jino, no, no!' cries his sister, but baby Jino just gurgles happily.

A skiff goes by, a ramshackle little wooden boat poled along by boys of fifteen and sixteen. Their bodies are smooth and lithe, supple with growing muscle. The three girls pretend to take no notice of the boys as they ride by, but each is secretly watching them, wondering.

'If you could have just one wish,' says Jeevamani to her friends, 'what would you ask for?'

Before either Parvati or Roshana can think about it, let alone answer, Jeevamani tells them what her wish would be. 'I'd have wings.' She stretches her arms out to the side. In her mind they are covered with beautiful feathers, white as snow.

Roshana disagrees. 'Great big wings sticking out all over the place, knocking things over,' she says. 'You wouldn't be able to sit down properly. You wouldn't fit behind the desks.'

'If you had wings, you wouldn't have to go to school,' counters Jeevamani. 'You would be famous. People would come and take your photograph, and write stories about you in magazines. They would pay you money to see you fly.'

Roshana asks Parvati, 'What about you?'

'I would wish for an end to war and hunger,' says Parvati passionately.

'That's two wishes!' cries Jeevamani.

'My father says all wars are caused by hunger,' replies Parvati resolutely.

'Well, then, all you need to do is wish for no more hunger,' Jeevamani tells her. 'Then there would be no more war.' She seems to think it important that her friend gets the terms of her wish straight now, just in case a goddess rises out of the river to grant it. 'If I had wings I could fly up and rescue little children from burning buildings,' she adds virtuously, as if conscious that her own wish seems a bit selfish beside Parvati's. 'What about you, Roshana?'

Roshana steers Jino's battered old pushchair carefully over exposed tree roots. 'I would wish for my Appa back again,' she says. She sounds so sad, the other girls fall silent, forgetting all thoughts of wings and war.

In a little while the three friends reach the point where the river widens and flows into a pool. They are expecting to meet two of Jeevamani's sisters there, the little ones, Mandri and Shanely. The water here is thick and soupy with mud. The level has gone down several centimetres since the girls last walked this way. Withered yellow reeds stick out of cracks in the dusty banks. Even the trees look thirsty.

Around the pool several hundred people are sitting,

chattering, singing, squabbling. Jeevamani starts looking
for her sisters. Every single scrap of shade has been
claimed by somebody. Sellers of sweetmeats and cool
drinks pick their way through the crowd. Trade is brisk.
In the muddy pool, animals are drinking, cows and dogs
and buffalo. Children are bathing, racing up and down in
the shallows splashing each other. Women are washing
pots and clothes. A smell of sweat and spice and incense
hangs in the burning air.

There is no hope of locating Mandri and Shanely. The
three friends decide not to stop but press on to the foot-
bridge. They work their way around the edge of the
babbling crowd. Jeevamani is carrying Jino now. Good-
hearted Parvati is pushing the empty pushchair. Roshana
wanders along, thinking of nothing. As they leave the
crowd behind, she looks up through the branches of the
trees, into the hard blue sky. She tries to remember what a
cloud looks like.

'Smita's boyfriend is writing a song about her,' Jeevamani tells them idly.

Parvati frowns. 'Arun? Writing a song?'

'Not *Arun*!' exclaims Jeevamani, jiggling Jino up and
down. 'Her *new* boyfriend!' Her manner is intense. Her
eyes flash from side to side of the river, on the lookout for
spies who might be trying to overhear her confidences.

So Jeevamani's big sister has a new secret boyfriend.
Jeeva seems to think her friends already ought to know
about him, nevertheless.

'Who is this one?' asks Parvati. 'What does he do?' She
sounds a bit cross. Though she hardly knows Jeevamani's
sister Smita and has certainly never met Arun, she seems
to resent his fall from favour.

Jeevamani sticks her nose in the air. Baby Jino pats her

on the chin. 'He is a musician,' Jeeva says. 'He composes his own songs. He is extremely talented.'

'I thought Smita and Arun were in love,' says Parvati, unwilling to give up Smita Anjumbandare's previous passionate predicament.

'Not like Smita and Anand,' retorts Jeevamani, boastfully. She seems to believe some kind of glory is reflected on her from the power of her sister's adoration.

Parvati seems satisfied with that. She does not welcome Jeevamani's announcement of a new claimant to her sister's hand; but she can see how a minstrel singing songs of love might be preferable to a deckhand covered in grime and engine oil.

Roshana is more suspicious. 'If he's that good, I suppose he's rich and famous,' she says.

'He drives a taxi,' says Jeevamani, irritated at being forced to confess it. '*For the moment.* You can't just be a musician until you're *discovered*.' She is an expert now, it seems, on the artistic life and its attendant difficulties.

'Oh, your Amma and Appa will love him!' says Parvati sarcastically.

Baby Jino has no idea what the girls are talking about, but he can feel perfectly well that their attention is no longer on him. He shows signs of starting to fret, throwing himself from side to side in Jeevamani's arms.

Roshana takes her brother from Jeevamani. 'He lives in the city, too, I suppose, this Anand,' she says.

'No, no. He lives here! Near the cinema,' says Jeevamani, pointing impatiently back towards the town. 'Rakhi Street, somewhere there.'

'But poor Arun!' says Parvati, sentimentally.

Jeevamani rolls her eyes. She starts to giggle. 'Arun doesn't know yet! Smita's afraid to tell him!'

Parvati thinks that is very wrong of Smita. Jeevamani disagrees. Parvati starts to tell Jeeva what her sister ought to do.

While her friends stroll on ahead along the riverbank, organizing Smita Anjumbandare's love-life for her, Roshana Kemal crouches down to force Jino's plump little legs beneath the front strap of his pushchair. Jino kicks vigorously, objecting to this treatment. He starts to grizzle. Roshana moans. 'Come *on*, Jino, be a *good boy*, please, please!' She feels close to tears herself. It is too hot, she is too tired, everything is too much today.

'My life would be so much easier without you!' she tells baby Jino viciously.

She will never be in love or have a boyfriend, she knows. Anyway, love just means trouble, she thinks grimly, conquering her struggling brother and tightening his straps. Trouble for people who have done nothing at all to deserve it.

Chapter 13

When Roshana gets home, Jino is fast asleep with his thumb in his mouth, his face squashed against the side of the pushchair. She pushes him into the garden, into the shade of a palm tree. Quietly she finds the piece of brick she uses to wedge the wheel. The brake is rusty and not very reliable.

Rajah has declared his intention of buying Jino a new pushchair, but Amma said it wasn't worth it. 'He likes his pushchair,' she told him, bouncing Jino, tipping him over backwards in her arms. 'Don't you, my precious? Really, darling, it will see him through. He'll be too big for a pushchair in a little while. He'll be running around on his own two feet, won't you, Jino, won't you just? Ooh, yes he will, *yes* he will, such a big boy he's getting.'

Rajah was not pleased. He made fun of Amma for her attachment to a worn-out piece of rubbish. All the time, though, he recognized the upbringing of her own children as one of the areas for which his new wife should have the principal responsibility, and he soon surrendered to her, extravagantly, with much praise for his own generosity in always giving her her own way. Since then, he grimaces when he happens to catch sight of

Jino's pushchair, and shouts for Roshana to come and put it away.

This afternoon Rajah is in the living room, sitting at the dining table with a cigarette and a glass of beer. He has his glasses on, and he's surrounded by piles of papers with numbers on them. He has not heard Roshana come in.

Roshana loiters in the doorway. 'Where's Amma?' she says.

Rajah glances up and down again. 'Hello, sweetheart,' he says, in a rumbling, preoccupied voice. 'Your mother's in bed. She's sleeping.'

Roshana starts to turn towards the stairs. 'I'll just—'

'You're not to disturb her,' orders her stepfather. 'She's not feeling very well.'

That's something else that happens a lot these days. It used to be that when Amma felt unwell, she would simply labour on. Even when she was carrying Jino and being sick all the time she would drag herself across to the factory, looking washed-out and ghastly. 'I have to, Roshi,' she would say, if ever Roshana tried to persuade her to stay at home and rest. 'That's all there is to it.'

Now, she takes to her bed at the slightest excuse. She lies there with the curtains drawn, surrounded by magazines and sweet wrappers.

Rajah runs his finger along a line of print. He sucks on his cigarette. Little twin horns of smoke curl from between his lips and go up his nose.

'You're wearing your glasses,' Roshana says.

He frowns at her. 'What of it?' he says, stiffly.

Roshana runs her finger down the moulding around the door. The paint is white and shiny. 'You don't wear them, usually,' she says idly.

Rajah returns to his work. 'I don't need them,' he says brusquely.

Roshana waits a moment. 'Why are you wearing them now, then?' she says.

'I only need them for reading,' Rajah declares.

Her stepfather doesn't like wearing his glasses. Roshana knows that. He seems to think they made him look old, or silly, or something. They're very smart glasses, in fact, expensive ones, of course, with big, bold lenses and slender gold frames. Still Rajah dislikes them, and avoids putting them on whenever he can. He is always forgetting where he's put them, and making a fuss about being unable to find them. Roshana finds it interesting to see how much Rajah's glasses vex him.

'You're always reading,' she tells him, relentlessly. 'Even when you're on the phone you—'

Rajah loses patience with her. 'Don't bother me, Roshana!' he shouts. 'Can't you see I'm busy? This is important work I'm doing here. This is what I have to do to put food on the table and clothes on your back. Now I must get the doctor to your mother, and you know how much *that* will cost.'

Roshana has no idea how much it costs to have the doctor. How should *she* know? All Rajah ever thinks about is money, she tells herself, and he thinks it should be all everyone else ever thinks about too.

Amma really is sick, though, she discovers when in a little while she sneaks upstairs and tiptoes into her room. The curtains are closed. Amma lies wrapped in her big shawl in a crumpled heap of bedclothes, but there are no sweeties in sight, nor any magazines. A smouldering joss stick fills the air with perfume.

'Hello, darling,' says her mother in a croaky voice. Her

face against the white pillows looks dark green. 'Did you have a nice walk with your friends?'

'What's the matter, Amma?' Roshana asks her. 'Is it your head?'

Her mother nods exhaustedly. 'My head, my stomach, my arms and legs are all pins and needles.' She gropes listlessly towards her night-table.

'Rajah says the doctor is coming,' says Roshana.

'My throat is burning up . . .'

Roshana locates the glass she is reaching for and puts it in her hand. Weakly her mother brushes the hair back from her daughter's forehead, smiling her thanks. 'Don't come too close, sweetheart, we don't want you catching this, whatever it is.'

Roshana twists her feet round until the toes of her left foot meet the toes of her right. She wants to fling herself into Amma's arms and hug her. She feels as if that would surely make her better.

'Where is your brother?'

'Sleeping,' says Roshana. 'Outside.'

'Bring him in, he must not lie so long in the sun.'

'I put him under a tree, Amma!' Roshana is exasperated. Ill Amma may be, but she ought to credit her daughter with *some* sense.

Amma's eyes close, her face creases up with pain. 'Gently, Roshi, my poor head!'

Roshana is unhappy. Amma was perfectly well yesterday, and this morning, when she asked her to take Jino out. Now she looks as ill as Roshana has ever seen her. Roshana reaches up and feels her forehead. It is hot and damp. Beneath the wafting fragrance of the incense she can smell the sour smell of sickness.

'Can I get you anything, Amma?'

'No, darling, thank you.'

'I'll get you fresh water.'

Amma's eyes close again. 'Bring Jino in now,' she says. 'He must have his tea.'

Going slowly downstairs, Roshana wonders how on earth Amma can think about food at all when she's ill.

She brings Jino indoors. He is wide awake, chattering happily. Roshana wipes his hands and face and puts him in his high-chair. By the time she has fastened the straps that keep him there, Amma is downstairs, tottering around in her big shawl.

'Fetch your father,' Amma tells Roshana. Wearily she sits by Jino, stirring a bowl of mash.

Jino doesn't want to cooperate. He keeps turning his face away from the spoon. Amma is too sick to battle with him. She struggles to her feet.

Rajah sits on Amma's other side, stuffing food into himself. When Amma gets up, he clamours at her. 'You shouldn't keep getting up, Jyoti! Let Roshana do it, whatever it is!'

Amma sits there with pain in her eyes, the corners of her mouth drawn down like a catfish. She does not want Rajah to shout at her. She just wants to be left alone.

Roshana gets up. She fetches Jino's bottle from the warmer and goes to give it to him. She moves deliberately between Amma and Rajah, ignoring her stepfather, treating him as if he were just a big piece of furniture.

Chapter 14

That night, Roshana Kemal dreams she is at the market. It is very crowded, exactly as it is in real life. People jostle her continually, keeping her from the stalls. Distantly, she hears the cry of the traders, calling coconuts, kulfi, sherbet, *Coca-Cola*.

Suddenly she finds herself in front of a fruit stall. All the people seem to have disappeared for a moment. Behind the stall a light-skinned girl is calling out to her, offering her yellow melons, green mangoes.

Like every other market-seller, the girl claims that her fruit is the best in the world. Yet all the fruit Roshana can see is obviously bad.

The girl is insistent. Roshana must buy her mangoes. She turns them over in their trays, showing her the undersides. Roshana sees each one is cratered with horrible wet black rot.

She would like to leave, but she understands that there are more mangoes behind the stall, in some sort of warehouse, Will they be bad too, or fresh and luscious? Does she want to go in, further in, or will she simply get further into difficulties?

From under the stall comes a dog. It is a scrawny black

mongrel. It is Nula, Rajah's parents' dog, the one that made a nuisance of itself when they went to visit them in the village in the mountains. Roshana backs away.

The dog is still with her. It is snarling, drooling. The sound of its barking hurts her ears.

Roshana is angry and afraid. She is sure the dog means to attack her. *I'll kill you!* she shouts at the black dog. She shouts it over and over again. *I'm going to kill you!*

Suddenly there seem to be two dogs. Now Roshana is horrified. Two dogs: the mean black one, and another one with short yellow fur and spots. Between them they will surely eat her up. Roshana feels a great aching sadness in her chest.

But the spotted dog is not after her. Instead, it seems to be after Nula, the black bitch. The spotted dog lowers its muzzle and growls. It nips Nula's ankles. It snaps at her flanks.

Roshana sees the spotted creature's big, pointed ears, its heavy, bushy tail. It comes to her, as if whispered on a breath of wind, that she has seen it before and that it is not a dog. She knows it means her no harm.

She sees Nula try to fight. Then she sees her defeated. Nula is yelping, cringing, lowering her ears. She is turning tail, fleeing, vanishing.

In the dream, a voice cries out gladly. Roshana has no idea whether it is her own.

'*Sivalu!*'

On that cry, Roshana wakes. Her heart is racing. She lies with her eyes shut tight, scarcely daring to open them.

The night is hot and still. Roshana hears the sound of her baby brother whimpering in his sleep.

She knows she has been dreaming. She remembers the

rotting fruit. The smell of it is still there in the back of her throat. It makes her feel sick to think of it.

She does not remember the black dog, or the jackal that chased it away.

Roshana thinks of Amma, and how ill she is. Her dream. She is convinced her dream was about Amma. The mangoes that had the rot in them: that was Amma and the sickness inside her.

Roshana thinks of Amma lying there in bed. She thinks of Rajah lying beside her, the great bulk of him. She imagines Amma engulfed in the powerful scent of his pomade. She feels a terrible helplessness.

Chapter 15

Roshana is on the floor of the dining room, playing with baby Jino. They are playing with Jino's train.

Jino's train is made of brightly coloured plastic. There is an engine, a truck and a carriage. The engine has a smiling face, and a funnel that bobs up and down. The engine driver is a pink pig in dungarees and a blue cap. Roshana thinks he looks quite sly, though that was probably not the intention of the manufacturers. In the truck there used to be six plastic building blocks, but they are gone, scattered long ago. Inside the carriage are two laughing monkeys in sailors' uniforms, holding up little flags.

Jino likes to chew the engine of his train. When he's not chewing it, he likes Roshana to pull it along the floor and make train noises. 'Whoo-whoo!' goes Roshana, on her hands and knees. She makes chuffing noises, blowing air out of her cheeks. As the engine goes along, the funnel bobs and the pig wags stiffly from side to side, looking now out of this side of the cab, now out of that. Jino warbles happily, bouncing up and down. When the train comes towards him, he spots the pig peeking out at him and squeals in delight.

Roshana doesn't mind having Jino this morning.

Though she has plenty of homework, she'd rather be here on the floor, frankly, pulling a little plastic train along. She doesn't believe she could concentrate on anything more taxing. Roshana had a nasty dream last night, about someone trying to sell her bad fruit. It was so unpleasant it woke her up, and she's not sure she ever got properly back to sleep.

When the doorbell rings Roshana drops the train, scoops up her brother and hurries to answer it. She could very well leave Jino to play on his own for a moment, but she wants him with her. She feels the need to protect him today. Or perhaps it is herself she is protecting.

At the door is a small woman in a smart grey skirt and a white blouse. She is wearing a powerful quantity of make-up, and a bright red *puttu* in the centre of her forehead. Her face is young, but her hair is iron-grey, and cut very short. Behind her is a small blue car, and beside her on the step a case made of shiny black leather.

'Good morning,' she says briskly. 'I am Dr Goenka. I am here to see Mrs Chowdry.'

For a second, Roshana doesn't recognize the name. She is about to tell the woman she has come to the wrong house and send her away. Then she remembers that Chowdry is Amma's new name, since she married Rajah. It is her own name too, of course, though she decided at once and for always that she would never use it.

'Come in,' says Roshana. 'She's upstairs. She's not very well,' she adds, foolishly.

The woman smiles crisply, picking up her case and stepping over the threshold. 'So I understand,' she says. Her voice is metallic too, like her hair. Jino, in Roshana's arms, crows loudly and waves and kicks. 'Good morning to you too, young man,' says Dr Goenka.

Rajah appears from somewhere, filling the hall with anxiety. He pulls a large handkerchief from the pocket of his cream linen suit and wipes his perspiring brow. 'Doctor, doctor, thank you for coming. I am Mr Chowdry. This way, please.' He bows as best he can, waving Dr Goenka towards the stairs.

The doctor strides past Roshana and Jino in a wave of surgical spirit. All the way upstairs Rajah blusters at her, giving her the benefit of his own opinion.

Roshana and Jino return to the train. It travels an ambitious route, under the table and over the chairs. It runs up Jino's left leg, over the top of his head and down his right arm. But the train has lost Jino's attention. Roshana tries a ball, a woolly lion, a fluffy duckling. 'Look! It's Ducky! Jino loves Ducky . . .' Jino is fretful now, unwilling to be entertained. He sucks his fingers and puts them in Roshana's hair, grizzling. He wants to be picked up, then he wants to be put down again. Roshana carries him to and fro. Even in the hall, she can hear only the faintest sounds from upstairs.

Shortly the doctor comes down, followed by Roshana's stepfather. She comes into the living room and looks at Roshana as if she suspects her of something. 'And your daughter, Mr Chowdry,' she says in her iron voice. 'How has she been? Any problems there?'

Roshana is annoyed at being referred to as Rajah's daughter. She doesn't see why the doctor is talking about her as if she weren't there. 'I'm perfectly all right, thank you,' she says loudly.

Without asking, the doctor reaches for Roshana's hand and takes her pulse. 'No nausea, headaches, fever?'

Roshana takes her hand back again. 'No,' she says.

The doctor lowers her eyelids. 'Put out your tongue,

please,' she orders. 'That seems to be all right.' She takes a smart black pen from her pocket and pulls off the cap.

Of course it's all right, thinks Roshana. I'm not the one who's ill, Amma is. Jino is on the floor, pressed against her leg. Roshana bends down to pick him up. His train comes with him, dangling from his hand.

'How are you sleeping?' asks Dr Goenka.

For an instant, Roshana freezes. She doesn't know if she wants to tell this metal woman about her disturbed nights, her dreams of leather-faced men and rotten fruit. She certainly won't while Rajah's standing there, listening to it all.

'Oh, fine,' she says carelessly. 'Very well.'

The doctor smiles at Jino, opening her eyes very wide. Jino is chewing the funnel of his engine. 'And there's nothing wrong with *you*, is there,' says Dr Goenka, taking hold of his toes and giving his foot a shake. The carriage and the truck come uncoupled from Jino's engine. They fall to the floor with a soft clatter.

The doctor is taking a prescription pad from her case.

'As I told your wife, Mr Chowdry, it's probably only a tummy bug. But just to be sure, I should like you to make a complete list of everything she has eaten in the last four days.'

Rajah huffs and puffs. 'Of course. Of course.' He is trying to look as though he is giving the matter serious consideration. Obviously, he hasn't the least idea what Amma has been eating, even though he ate it too, five times as much of it as Amma did, in all probability. 'Roshana will do that for you,' he says.

'Oh, yes, Roshana will do it,' murmurs Roshana, sarcastically.

'You're to help your mother now, Roshi!' trumpets her stepfather sternly.

Dr Goenka writes on her pad. While she is writing, nobody speaks. The only sound in the room is the scratching of her pen on the paper. Even Jino is dumb, awed by the smart woman with the crimson mouth.

Dr Goenka tears off the prescription and hands it to Rajah. 'Three times a day for seven days,' she says.

Roshana takes the paper. 'I know, I know. Roshana will fetch it,' she says, and without another word she carries Jino off to the other end of the house, his engine still firmly in his mouth. She dumps him unceremoniously in his pushchair, and straps him in.

The nearest chemist is a ten-minute walk away. Going down the hill Roshana sees a magazine that someone has dropped. Sophisticated fashion models pout at the sky, unaware they have been soiled and trampled. An old man goes past on a bicycle, riding very, very slowly. Jino sings tunelessly, rocking from side to side like the engine-driving pig.

When they get to the chemist's, Roshana parks her brother out of the sun, under an iron staircase. She checks to see the pushchair won't roll away.

'Now you be good, Jino. I won't be a minute.' The shop is small, and crammed with stock, shelves high and low full of bottles and packets. Jino would have everything over in seconds.

Inside the shop, the air is hot, and stirred by a large electric fan. It smells of a thousand clean scents, peppermint and sulphur and carbolic soap. A stout woman and her daughter are at the counter, fussing over an assortment of skin creams that an assistant is laying out for them.

An old woman comes to serve Roshana. The chemist's mother, she must be, or his mother-in-law. She takes the prescription and disappears into the back of the shop. Roshana looks around at all the things on the shelves, the coloured boxes of drugs, the rubber gloves in bunches like pink bananas, the hairnets secretive and spidery in their cellophane packets.

The stout woman and her daughter have decided that none of the creams is at all suitable. They squeeze their way out into the sunshine, arguing loudly. Then the chemist emerges from the back room, with his white coat and his thick spectacles, his professional, froglike smile. 'Tell your mother, three times a day for seven days,' he says to Roshana, putting a brown bottle in a white paper bag and giving it to her.

Roshana comes out of the shop. The sun is blazing down. Jino has gone, pushchair and all.

Chapter 16

The police have talked to Roshana. There was a woman constable, and then a pair of plain-clothes detectives: a woman with a face like a hatchet and a man who hardly spoke to Roshana but only to the woman, in a low, dull voice. Roshana doesn't think she gave them much help. She still feels confused, stupid, as if all the guilt was welling up from her heart into her head and stopping her from thinking straight.

Amma blames her. Roshana is sure she does. Though she hugged her, sobbing, saying over and over again that it wasn't her fault, Roshana knows it was. She thinks of all the time she wasted running up and down the street, grabbing the arms of bewildered passers-by and shouting at them, 'Have you seen a little boy in a pushchair? A little baby, this big, with a toy engine?' Nobody had. Many of them brushed her away and strode on, refusing to listen. Then Roshana wasted more time by running all the way back to the shop and trying to tell the chemist, who was too busy serving to pay attention to her and kept saying, 'Just one minute, there, please. Just one minute.' In the end the old woman impelled her outside and questioned her thoroughly before finally agreeing to go back in and phone the police.

Utterly spent, Roshana takes herself off to bed. She is sure she is too wound up to sleep but she drops off immediately, and wakes again, in darkness. If she has been dreaming, she doesn't know what it was about. She doesn't remember anything.

Out of the darkness a strange ghostly light produces the shapes of furniture. It stands a line of books on the shelf and drapes clothes over the chair. The treacherous light makes them all look as if they were someone else's things, smuggled in while Roshana slept.

That light is coming from outside. Only partly aware of what she is doing, Roshana slips out of bed and goes to the window.

There is someone out there, under the trees. By the size of him, Roshana immediately recognizes her stepfather Rajah. He has a powerful electric lantern with him. He seems to be digging in the earth.

Suddenly afraid, though of what she could by no means explain, Roshana goes quickly into the bedroom Rajah shares with her mother.

It is dark in there. On the far side of the double bed, Roshana makes out her baby brother's cot. She goes around to look inside it. It is still empty.

In the bed is Amma, fast asleep. A slim brown glint on the night-table is the brown glass bottle Roshana fetched her from the chemist's. 'Amma,' she calls, softly. 'Amma!' Her mother only sighs and mutters in her drugged sleep.

The blood singing in her ears, Roshana gallops downstairs and straight out into the garden.

Her stepfather is already knee deep in a hole in the ground. Beside the hole lies something bundled up in a black plastic bag, something no more than a metre long. It lies there on the ground, unmoving.

Roshana is filled with terror. 'What are you doing?' she cries.

Rajah looks at her sadly. In a quiet, defeated voice he says, 'Go back to bed, sweetheart.'

It is so strange to see him like this, with mud all over his trousers, working like a labourer. It makes no sense at all that he is doing it in the garden, in the middle of the night. The whole thing is as weird as one of Roshana's weird dreams.

'What are you *doing*?' she cries again. '*What have you got in that bag?*'

She darts for the bundle. Her stepfather tries to stop her. She bites him on the hand. He jerks away from her. Roshana sees how hard he is breathing. There is perspiration running down his cheeks.

She seizes hold of the bag. Her hands sense the shape of something inside it, something firm and narrow and bony. It must be an arm or a leg.

'It's Jino!' she yells, full of righteous accusation. 'You poisoned Amma and now you've killed Jino!' With her fingernails she tears the shiny black fabric.

Inside is a dog. It is the dog she keeps dreaming about, Nula, the black mongrel bitch from the mountains. Her fur is matted, her lips drawn back from her yellow teeth. Her eyes are open, gleaming golden in the lantern-light, staring. The smell of her is disgusting. She is quite dead.

Distantly, Roshana hears her stepfather say, 'Leave her now, can't you? Just leave her alone.'

Roshana stares. What is the dog doing here? How did it die? She feels dazed and weary.

'It was your family's dog,' she hears herself say.

'She loved me best,' Rajah says. 'In the end.'

Roshana realizes he is weeping. Suddenly, she is over-powered by shame and despair.

A voice calls from the house. It is Roshana's amma. Their quarrel has roused her from the depths of sedation.

'What is all this noise? Roshana, is that you? What are you doing out of bed?'

Roshana does not know how to answer. She looks at her sweating stepfather, at the wretched defunct animal in its shroud of torn polythene. She feels herself start to weep too.

Chapter 17

Roshana has to go to school. Though she would much rather stay at home, Rajah will not hear of it. 'I shall be here,' he says, lighting more incense for Ganesh. 'I shall look after your mother. I will let you know at once if there's any news. The best thing you can do, Roshi, is to go and work hard. Study hard for those exams!'

Any other day, Roshana would have argued. Today, she feels too demoralized, too unsure of herself. Rajah keeps pacing up and down, smoking, looking out of the front door as if expecting every minute to see a messenger hurrying up the road with a ransom demand, or even a rescuer wheeling his baby stepson home. He does not mention the dog. Roshana has seen from her bedroom window the pathetic little mound that now covers it, under the palm trees.

At Blessed Nativity, everybody has heard about Jino. Sister Immaculata leads the whole school in prayer. 'Mother Mary, for the love of Lord Jesus thy son, look down we beseech you on little Jino Chowdry. Keep him safe, Holy Mother, and guide the feet of all the good people out looking for him today . . .'

Parvati and Jeevamani are kind to Roshana. They stay with her, fending off everyone who crowds round with questions. Some of the others keep away from her, and even avoid meeting her eye. Roshana notices. It is as if they are afraid of catching her bad luck.

Jeevamani is angry. 'They're all talking about you, even if they pretend they're not!'

'Shut up, Jeeva!' says Parvati. She is close to tears herself, all day. She twists a damp handkerchief between her hands. 'The poor little baby . . .' she whispers.

Later in the day, Sister Immaculata takes Roshana to one side. 'You must be a brave girl,' she says. 'We are all praying for you and your family.'

Roshana looks at the sister's long face. It is as white as the belly of a fish.

'Sister,' she asks, 'do dreams come true?'

Sister Immaculata looks at her intelligently. 'The Holy Bible tells us our Heavenly Father sent messages to His prophets in their dreams. You remember, don't you, Pharaoh's dream, the seven thin cows that ate up the seven fat ones!'

Roshana hasn't a clue what Sister Immaculata is talking about. What cows were those?

Sister Immaculata takes Roshana's smooth brown hands in her own, which are pale and narrow, and chilly, despite the heat of the day. Sister Immaculata smells faintly of cold cream.

'A wise man once said dreams are a mask on the face of the truth.'

Roshana becomes frightened. In her mind's eye she sees the face of the Shadowman: his vast turban, his black-lipped smile.

Sister Immaculata's face is full of love and pity for her

little pupil. 'Roshana, darling heart, what is it? Have you had a dream about little Jino, is that it?'

Roshana lifts her chin. Outside in the playground she can hear the sound of chanting. Sister Martha is teaching the little girls a song.

'It was about a dog,' Roshana murmurs. 'A dog that Rajah's family had.'

'Your stepfather, that is,' says Sister Immaculata.

'It was a horrible dog, all dirty and skinny. It had great long yellow teeth.' Roshana finds herself staring at Sister Immaculata's teeth, which are quite long too, and very yellow. 'It wouldn't leave me alone.'

'In the dream, is this, now?' asks the puzzled nun.

Roshana shakes her head. 'We went to see them,' she says. She thinks she will burst into tears if the sister doesn't understand. 'It kept barking at us,' she says. 'It kept sniffing me. It was horrible.' Roshana hears the words coming out of her mouth. She sounds like a little girl.

Sister Immaculata looks as if she'd like to bring this to a conclusion. 'I expect the dream was just a bad memory,' she starts to say.

Roshana continues, ignoring her. 'In the dream I told the dog I was going to kill it,' she says.

'Ah, now, Roshana, we're not responsible for the things we do in our dreams . . .'

'I wished it dead,' Roshana says. 'And now it is. It is dead. In real life.'

Sister Immaculata seems confused. Roshana feels worn out and shivery. She can't tell the sister her true fear, which is that baby Jino has been taken away as a punishment, because she killed the dog.

At that instant Rajah appears, coming along the hallway. He has overheard the end of their conversation. 'She was an old dog,' he tells Sister Immaculata, dismissing the topic. 'Not in the best of health. Very sad, but what can you do? Her time had come, that's the truth of it.'

Rajah says he has come to take his stepdaughter home. Roshana just gazes at him. It is strange to see him here at Blessed Nativity. He has never come here before. He does not fit inside these walls. His size seems to threaten the entire building, as if the floor might collapse under his weight.

Rajah is holding out his hand. 'The car is outside,' he tells Roshana.

'Have they found him?'

Her stepfather shakes his head. His eyes are hooded, brooding. Roshana thinks of the brown glass bottle on Amma's night-table.

On the way home, Roshana almost falls asleep. She knows she is in the car, riding along, but she has the impression that people are talking to her, sometimes several people at once. They seem to be giving her instructions, lists of things she is supposed to do; but she doesn't know who they are and she can't hear a word they're saying. She tries to jump up and catch their words as they fly, but they are gone like the words of a song when the music comes to an end.

The Chrysler turns a corner, throwing Roshana against Rajah's side. She struggles to wake up and sit up straight.

Her stepfather is speaking. 'She must have followed me home,' he says. 'She got here, though it killed her.'

His voice is mournful, though there is pride in it. For a moment Roshana has no idea who he is talking about. Then she realizes he means the dog.

There are cars and vans parked all down Kosala Road,

both sides. Lights flash as Roshana gets out of the car. People are running towards her, shouting at her, pointing cameras and tape recorders at her.

Her stepfather holds his hand up, motioning them all to keep back. 'No comment,' he says loudly, over and over. 'No comment. Let us through, please.' He shields her as he shepherds her indoors. For once, Roshana is grateful for his girth.

The house is full of police again: the detectives who were there before, along with more uniformed men and women than Roshana can count.

Amma is in bed with a wet towel over her eyes. 'They want to talk to you again, darling,' she moans. 'Wring my towel out for me, before you go, there's a good girl.'

Roshana soaks the towel with cold water, wrings it out and puts it back over Amma's eyes. Then she goes down to talk to the police, who ask her the same questions they asked before. What time exactly did she last see baby Jino? Was there anyone hanging about, anyone suspicious, anyone at all?

Roshana gives them the same answers. She doesn't object, though it is obvious they are getting nowhere. The police still have no idea where Jino is, who took him, or why.

Chapter 18

The Shadowman is talking to Roshana, trying to coax her through a doorway. He is holding out a shiny black feather. *Take it*, he says. His voice is warm and friendly. Still Roshana continues to resist.

The Shadowman laughs. Suddenly, Roshana's clothes are full of feathers. There are feathers in her pockets, up her sleeves, inside her blouse. She tries to get rid of them. She starts pulling them out in handfuls. There seems to be no end to them. They cling to her hands. They get caught inside her sleeves. She is half smothered in feathers. There are feathers in her mouth, up her nose. She can hear the Shadowman laughing and laughing. She will never trust him, never, she thinks; and with that she wakes and finds herself in bed.

There is light in her room again. This time it is not coming from the window. It is coming from the door. The door of her bedroom is open. Someone is standing outside, looking in at her.

It is not the Shadowman. It is not a detective, or a newspaper reporter. It is her stepfather, Rajah.

Roshana is alarmed to see him there. Something must

be wrong. Jino is dead. Amma is dead. The world is coming to an end. The house is burning down.

She will not speak. She will not let him see that she is awake. She lies and listens to her heart thump. She lies peeing through her eyelashes, waiting to see what he will do.

He does nothing. He stands there looking at her, a vast silhouette blotting out the landing light. Roshana can smell his sweet pomade.

She turns her head away. She no longer cares whether or not he knows she is awake. Let him come in and murder her. The way she feels now, Roshana is not even sure she would bother to defend herself.

Chapter 19

Roshana lies in bed with the sun coming through the curtains. She has just woken up. It is already nearly ten.

The figures on the face of the clock mean nothing to her. She feels tired and stupid and conquered. She can see no reason to get up, so she lies there, wishing she were still asleep.

She wonders if the reporters and photographers are still outside the house, waiting for her to show her face. Probably they are, she thinks. She wonders how long it will take them to get bored and go away. She wishes they would. She can't imagine, really, why they've come. She has never wanted to be famous; never wanted to see herself on TV, or have her picture in the paper.

Thinking of which, Roshana puts her hand under her pillow and feels for the picture.

It's the picture that used to be on the wall in the caravan, the one of her with Appa and Amma in the meadow. She feels the need, now, to keep it hidden; as if somebody might come and steal that too.

It was Roshana's tenth birthday. In the picture, she's wearing a beautiful pink sari that Amma had made her specially, and lovely dangly earrings. She stands in long grass between Amma and Appa, holding one of each of their hands, striking an artful, provocative pose like one of Krishna's dancing maidens, and grinning a huge smug grin. There is a big flower in her hair, that Appa climbed up a tree to pick for her.

That was the last place they lived, where Appa worked in a timberyard. Where they were living was a horrible place, a hostel, with all kinds of rules and regulations, and people coming and going all night and day. There was a foul concrete staircase that you had to creep up and down under the eyes of the sullen young men who hung about there with their beer cans and cigarettes and ghetto-blasters playing *bhangra* music at ear-shattering volume. It seems a long time ago now.

In Roshana' picture, Amma has a funny expression on her face, proud and offended and laughing, all at the same time. She is pretending to be scandalized by Roshana's behaviour. Appa just looks happy. He is squinting in the sunlight and smiling through his beard.

The photo was taken by a friend of Appa's from work, who had brought his camera down to the river specially to find the little birthday girl. He was a lovely silly man with great big puppy eyes who'd made her laugh, and flirted with her as if she were a grown-up lady. Banu, his name was. It was for Banu that she was posing.

Listlessly, Roshana turns over. She wishes she were ten again, a little girl playing in a river meadow with her Amma and Appa, knowing nothing, unaware of all the things that were about to go wrong. Unaware of Appa's accident, of Amma meeting Rajah, marrying Rajah, falling ill. Unaware of the Shadowman.

She lies there listening. She thinks she hears baby Jino crying. Then she remembers. No Jino. Jino is gone.

Roshana remembers the dream she had about Yama, the Lord of the Dead. He was coming to claim a soul. Appa was there too, in the dream. Roshana had assumed it was Appa's soul Yama was there for, but of course she understands now. Yama had Appa's soul already.

It was Jino's soul the Death King was claiming.

Roshana thrusts her picture back under the pillow. Her heart is aching. She knows she will never smile again.

Chapter 20

'Roshana! Roshana! We saw you! We saw you last night!'

Jeevamani comes running into the classroom, almost tripping over in her haste. She barges through the knot of girls clustered around Roshana and comes to a rest leaning across the desk. From a distance of ten centimetres, she tells her friend:

'You were on the *telly*!'

Her voice rises to a squeak.

'Leave her *alone*, Jeeva!' says Parvati, her arm round Roshana's shoulders. 'Take no notice of her, Roshi!'

Roshana isn't really taking any notice of anything. She has come to school for the afternoon because they made her. She put on her clothes and got in the taxi, which Rajah had agreed to call for her, after arguing with her mother who said he should take her in the car.

Roshana had sat in the taxi and ridden through town feeling like a robot replica of herself. It had been a slow journey. They had had to stop on the corner by the Pathrose Bridge, where a great many boxes were being loaded on a lorry. While they waited, people crossing the road in front of them had stopped to peer into the taxi and point. Roshana gazed straight ahead through the windscreen, feeling nothing. When eventually they managed to get past the obstruction and were moving slowly ahead, the taxi driver had said suspiciously, 'Who are you, then? Why were they looking at you?' Roshana had not answered, and he had not spoken again.

Now she is here she feels no better and no worse. She has begun to wish she were a robot replica, and the real Roshana was still at home, in bed, asleep.

'We all saw it,' Jeevamani continues, for the benefit of the gathering class. 'She was outside their house with her sittappa, and he opened the door and they went in. I knew it was your house, Roshi, I told everybody it was,' Jeeva declares proudly. 'They didn't know, I was the only one.'

Parvati yells. 'Jeeva!' She slaps her friend on the arm. 'Shut up!'

Jeevamani blinks, astonished, utterly lost for words. Parvati had slapped her! Parvati, who was always so gentle and quiet and never cross!

'He's still *missing*,' says Parvati fiercely to Jeevamani. 'They haven't found *anything*!'

Now Roshana is wishing Parvati would shut up.

Sister Charity arrives, making no comment at all on Roshana's arrival, but starting them immediately on English verbs, transitive and intransitive. The room is too small, the room is too hot, the press of bodies on the benches is the only thing holding Roshana upright. She turns over the pages when everyone else does and wishes she could die here and now, so as never to have to think or speak or do anything ever again.

By the time the end of the day eventually comes crawling along, Roshana's sudden fame seems to have worn itself out. There is the usual headlong exodus, everybody rushing out of the building as if it were about to explode. Roshana pushes with them for the doors.

Parvati clings to her. She seems to feel that Roshana is still rather in need of her protection. She is convinced of it when, outside, Roshana turns right instead of left.

'What are you doing now, Roshi?' asks Parvati, quite alarmed. 'Where are you going?'

Roshana looks as if she's walking in her sleep. She answers her friend dully. 'I'm going to look for him.'

This is the best idea Parvati has heard all day. 'I'll come with you!' she says. 'Hey, Jeeva, Jeeva, over here! Come with us, Roshana and me, we're going to look for Jino!'

Jeevamani looks disappointed and frustrated. She has her little sisters with her, Mandri and Shanely. Shanely is picking her nose. 'I can't come!' wails Jeevamani. Smita is due back from another visit to the city, apparently, and Jeeva has promised her mother to bring the little ones straight home.

Parvati obviously thinks this is too bad. Roshana doesn't really care whether anyone comes with her or not. She is desperate to be out there, doing something. More to the point, she simply can't face the idea of going home and doing her homework while Rajah blunders from room to room like an angry bullock and Amma lies upstairs in the darkness, out of touch, out of communication.

The town has never seemed more full of confusion. It is impossible even to cross the main road for jammed traffic. Somebody has left a van in the middle of the road, with the engine running and both doors open. Police, indignant motorists, passers-by with nothing better to do, have all converged on the van and are standing around it arguing. All around, frustrated drivers are sounding their horns as if they think the problem might best be solved by a simple increase in noise. As Roshana and Parvati squeeze through the crush, somebody manages to prise open the back doors of the abandoned van to reveal a load of chickens in crates, all squawking in terror.

Parvati hangs on to Roshana's hand. 'Where are we going first, Roshi?'

'Come on!' Roshana shouts back.

Pedestrians, dogs, sweating porters with barrowloads of rice, all seem to compete for the chance to get in the way of the two young girls as they struggle across the market and along the street towards the temple of Vishnu. Overhead, pigeons whirl round and round. The sky seems to press down from above, hot and blue and thick, as if you could reach up and thrust your arm in it up to the shoulder.

The way they are heading is nowhere near where Jino disappeared, thinks Parvati as they dodge a shouting man on a motorcycle. She feels sure Roshana has no idea where to look, but she is carried with her, obedient to her fury. Roshana frowns at every baby they pass, boy or girl, newborn or toddler, letting none of them escape her scrutiny. Babies that clutch toys particularly attract her attention, as if the merest rag doll or teething ring might be a clue to the whereabouts of the plastic engine.

Parvati tugs Roshana's arm. 'There!' she shouts over the noise. Roshana stops to look. Parvati is pointing down a shady alleyway. 'Isn't that Jino's pushchair?' she asks dramatically.

One glance tells Roshana her friend is wrong. The pushchair is new instead of old, blue rather than white, and fitted with a little canopy of yellow plastic printed with pictures of prancing, winking ponies. Nevertheless, she hurries into the alley and examines it; and when she has, turns to Parvati with an expression of disappointment.

'It's not his.'

Parvati hugs her. Roshana shrugs her off in a frenzy. There is no time for consolation. They have a hundred thousand babies to look at!

Eventually, tiring of dashing about the streets, the girls trail wearily towards the river, for no other reason than that it is a place they know. They wander along the path between the brittle, shrivelled undergrowth to the pool, calling as they go. *'Jino! Ji-no!'*

Beyond the pool stands the banyan tree. Its thousand branches spread an evergreen ceiling over its colonnade of soft grey trunks, magnificent natural shelter for birds and bats and monkeys. Pedlars have set up shop here, spreading their trinkets on lengths of grubby cloth. Beggars sit hugging themselves in the shade, smoking *chillums* and rocking to and fro on their skinny haunches, whining for alms as the two girls pass.

The sun goes down like an egg yolk brimming in blood; and even before it is gone gigantic fortresses of purple cloud are sighted, sailing out of the south-west.

At twenty minutes to midnight, the rain begins.

Chapter 21

Roshana lies in bed and listens to the rain fall on the roof of Rajah's white house. She hears it fall on the trees and bushes, on the soft mud heaped over the grave of the dead dog. She hears it gurgle into the drains of Kosala Road. In the distance, the wheels of cars hiss through the gathering water.

Soothed by the rhythm of the rain, Roshana slides bit by bit into sleep, and into a confused dream where the sound of the rain changes into the sound of the river, fatter now and brown, and rushing to the sea.

Roshana thinks she is beside the river, pushing through thick, tall undergrowth. She thinks she is trying to catch up with somebody. She can hear voices talking on the other side of the bushes, talking carelessly, laughing excitedly, always just out of sight. The dense shrubbery impedes her, catching her clothes, hitting her in the face. Every time another bush snares her, the hidden people seem to laugh more loudly, as if they find her difficulties amusing.

Now she is in the meadows, free of the bushes, and running through long grass towards a thicket of trees. The trees are huge. They reach right up to the purple sky, stretching, it seems, from horizon to horizon.

Even while she runs, Roshana knows that it is not really a thicket of trees, but only one tree – the banyan tree, which swallows everything it touches. From the branches of the banyan roots drop down, twisting in the air like hairy snakes, hungry for the soil; and where the roots nose into the rain-soaked ground, new trunks spring up, unstoppable and strong.

Roshana is in amongst the trunks of the banyan now, ducking and clambering through the twisting branches. The leaves of the banyan are long and thick and green. Roshana can see where things have been tied to the branches as offerings to the gods: bows of satin ribbon, little smiling mascots and painted dolls. Some of the dolls seem almost to be alive. They wave their tiny arms and cry. As Roshana scrambles past them she sees they are babies, infants, children – little girls and little boys, in all kinds of clothes, drab and colourful, rich and ragged.

Roshana's heart rises into her mouth. Frantically she starts to look for Jino.

She sees children of all colours, black, brown, yellow, white. She sees starving children with huge swollen tummies and pitiful eyes, and fat children that dangle from the branches of the banyan like ripe, juicy figs. There are grown-ups too, lurking in the gaps and shadows. They have been up here so long they are quite at home now. Roshana is convinced it was their voices, chatting and laughing, that she was following before.

On the topmost branch of the banyan is a big black bird, a giant crow. It spots Roshana climbing towards it. The crow spreads its wings and cries out in harsh displeasure; and Roshana wakes.

It is still raining, raining as if it has always rained, since the creation of the universe; raining as if it means never to stop. Roshana lies with her hands under her head and tries to remember her dream. She knows it was about the banyan again, the tree of trees, the tree of earth and sky in whose branches hang the stars of heaven. She doesn't know whether or not she saw him in the dream, but she is perfectly certain that that tree belongs to the Shadowman, and the people she saw among its branches were all the people he has stolen away.

Chapter 22

In the morning, it is still raining. When Roshana goes in to see how Amma is and if she needs anything, she finds her looking quite unhappy, with a screwed-up paper tissue stuffed in each ear. 'The rain kept me awake all night,' she says. Her voice is very weak and hoarse. She is clutching a cup of tea but not drinking it. As she kisses her mother goodbye Roshana can see the brown skin forming on the top of the cooling tea.

This morning Rajah is going to the office, and seems to think it would be all right for him to drive his stepdaughter to school. 'Hurry up, please, darling,' he says, shuffling papers into a briefcase and glancing at his big gold watch. 'I have a great deal to do.'

Roshana avoids him. She knows where the big umbrella is, and slips away to fetch it.

Rajah catches her as she is about to go out of the back door with it. 'What are you doing, child? Did I not just say I would take you to school today?'

Roshana gives him a nice smile, to disarm him. 'It'll be quicker walking,' she says, and for an instant she forgets and almost calls him *Appa*.

She doesn't really know if it will be quicker, but the

roads are full of water, and there are certain to be bad
traffic hold-ups. She simply doesn't want to have to sit in
the car with her stepfather. She can't help it. Whatever
Rajah wants, Roshana immediately wants the opposite.

Roshana walks out into the rain.

Mr Chowdry stands in the doorway with his hands
lifted out to either side, like a wrestler ready for a fight.
He calls after her.

'I'm not getting you a taxi again, if that's what you
think! Not when I'm driving . . .'

The storm washes his words away.

The big umbrella is red and yellow and blue, two panels
of each colour. With the rain hammering on it, it's as
much as Roshana can do to hold it up.

In the town the traffic is crawling. When it speeds up for
a moment, waves of thick, dusty water roll over the
pavement, soaking everyone's legs. Dogs trot about, nos-
ing excitedly at things afloat in the water. Cyclists weave
expertly in and out of the labouring cars with plastic bags
on their heads and their trouser legs rolled up.

At school it is chaos, as always on the first day of the
rains. The little girls run from room to room with their
arms stretched out, squealing. The nuns run behind them,
shouting ineffectually and clapping their hands.

Parvati comes in wrapped in an enormous waterproof
cape. Her face peeps from the hood like a camper looking
out of a tent. When she sees her friends she slips delicately
out of the cape, trying not to get any water on her. She
embraces Roshana. She wants news of Jino. 'Have they
found him yet?'

Roshana shakes her head. She doesn't want to think
about the fruitless search she and Parvati made yesterday
after school. 'They say they are following some promising

lines of inquiry,' she says. It is something she heard someone say once on a TV show.

Parvati clenches her fists in frustration. 'We looked *everywhere*!' she claims.

'Jino will turn up,' says Jeevamani, who is sitting on the windowsill. She doesn't like the thought that she couldn't help her friends search yesterday. She prefers to think there was no real need for them to wear themselves out looking under every stall in the marketplace and every bush along the riverbank. 'It's my sister I'm worried about,' she says carelessly.

'Smita?' says Parvati. 'What's the matter with her?'

Jeevamani fixes them with a dramatic look. 'She was supposed to come home last night,' she reminds them.

Parvati gives a little gasp. 'Where is she? Is she all right?'

Jeevamani opens her eyes wide. 'They don't know!' she says. She sounds as much cross as frightened. 'Mr Masulkur hasn't come home either!'

It appears that where the Anjumbandare city cousins live is a big block with only one payphone. Jeevamani's father has tried the number several times, late last night and this morning, but all he gets is silence.

Roshana looks out at the pouring rain. The phone lines are down, she thinks to herself. The roads are flooded. Even the trains will have difficulty getting through, today.

Meanwhile Parvati's mind is brimming over with disasters and wild imaginings. 'Perhaps something dreadful has happened to her!' she says, forgetting, in her excitement, that Roshana is there.

Jeevamani is perfectly prepared to think Parvati may be right. 'My aunt knew a woman whose next-door neighbour was killed by lightning,' she says lugubriously. 'And there was this farmer, on the telly, and his farm was flooded, so he had to go out in a boat to look after his animals, only the boat was old and it sank, and the man drowned in his own fields.'

Roshana agrees that the fates of these poor people were terrible. Privately, she thinks all that's happened to Smita Anjumbandare is that she's using the weather as an excuse to stay an extra day in the city with her boyfriend.

Smita is a bit mad, Roshana thinks. Her parents must be a bit mad too, sending someone like her to the city with only a dopey old man as her escort. That girl will come to no good, Roshana's amma is always saying. Roshana does not want to hurt her friend's feelings, so she says nothing.

It was Arun, though, Smita's old boyfriend, who lived in the city, Roshana remembers as Sister Martha comes into the room talking loudly, announcing the start of the lesson. Smita has a new boyfriend now, the singing taxi-driver, here in town. Roshana starts to understand why Jeevamani's frightened.

While everybody is shuffling into their places and opening their books, Roshana looks out of the window. The rain is still falling, the water rising. An empty plastic bottle floats down the street. Perhaps in a minute Jino's pushchair will float by too. Perhaps Jino will be riding in it, laughing and clapping his hands as he comes sailing along.

Roshana is quite sure the rain can't be hurting her brother. Whoever it was that took him, they took him because they wanted him, wanted him for themselves. They won't leave him outside in the rain.

That doesn't mean she will ever see him again, though.

Something suddenly runs down Roshana's face and drops, with a plop, on the page in front of her. It is a tear.

Chapter 23

It is morning again. It is still raining.

Amma is sitting up in bed, looking a little stronger. When she sees Roshana, she holds out her arms.

Roshana goes around the bed to hug her. As she passes the empty cot she notices something inside it, something little and round and greyish-yellow. It is the toy duckling that Jino loves. It gazes into space with a silly, happy expression.

Roshana hugs her mother. Amma is sitting quite up-right. She says she feels much better. In fact she is quite well.

'It is all your nursing!' Roshana hears her say. 'Without my little girl, I should have been lost!'

Roshana is uncomfortable. She starts to feel that she *is* a little girl, when Amma says that. She is a little girl who likes to play pretending games, like pretending to be a nurse.

Like all little girls who play games, and little boys too, Roshana always used to want the grown-ups to take hers seriously. Now that they are, now that Amma is saying she has done something important, Roshana feels that on the contrary, she is shameful and ridiculous. She starts to get cross. *I'm not a nurse!* she wants to say.

Roshana carries Amma's breakfast tray downstairs. Rajah is standing in the hall. He is waiting for her. 'Good morning, Roshana,' he says loudly. He seems to be in a good mood too. No doubt he is happy because Amma is better. He laughs. 'This rain will wash everybody's hands and faces clean!' he says.

He points out into the garden. It is a lake, with trees growing out of it. The trees are shiny green, heavy with water.

'We can swim to school today!' says Rajah.

Roshana is ready to quarrel with him, but she senses he has stopped trying to fight her. Her hostility evaporates; though she is nowhere near ready to give him a proper smile.

'I'll walk,' she says stiffly. 'I can walk.'

Suddenly, Rajah is holding up the big umbrella. Roshana didn't see where he produced it from or how he managed to put it up without her seeing.

He bows like a conjurer, or like the doorman at a grand hotel. He holds the umbrella over Roshana's head, and offers her the handle.

'Your umbrella, madam.'

Roshana is holding the umbrella. She is walking through the town. All around, the rain is still pouring, but down through the canopy of the umbrella a bright light is shining down on her, painting her body red and yellow and blue. Patches of colour bob away from her on the water, pouring across the road and cascading into the shops.

Now Roshana hears somebody else greet her gladly. 'A good morning to you, Mistress Roshana. What a beautiful day!'

Roshana looks around, and sees no one. She looks

down at her feet and sees an animal like a dog, with thick, spotted fur and big, pointed ears. The animal grins up at her and wags its heavy, bushy tail.

It is not a dog. It is Sivalu.

'Now I know I'm dreaming!' says Roshana.

Chapter 24

Sivalu the clever jackal runs around in a circle, snapping at the raindrops, chasing his own tail. He looks more like a dog than ever.

Roshana is a bit nervous of him, because he does look very much like a dog, and she doesn't like dogs; but also because he is a magical animal out of a fairy story. He shouldn't be here on the street, in the middle of town. But his antics make her laugh and she decides not to be frightened.

Sivalu splashes through the water around Roshana's feet. He gives himself a shake. Roshana holds out the umbrella to shield herself from the flying water.

Sivalu sticks his head under the umbrella and grins up at her.

'Where are we going this beautiful day, Mistress?'

This is getting worse! she thinks. 'I'm not your mistress, Sivalu!'

'Are we going to school?'

Roshana giggles. 'I can't take you to school!' she says. 'Sister Charity would have a fit!'

Sivalu doesn't seem to be offended. 'Where shall we go, then?' His voice is reedy, like someone talking through his nose, but it is musical too, lilting, enchanting.

Roshana looks into his wicked golden eyes. She is sure he has something in mind for her. It is like when a grown-up asks you a question not to find out the answer but to see if you know it; to see if you're clever enough to work it out. If only she knew what Sivalu is thinking!

Sivalu pants. 'Where would you most like to go, in the whole world?'

Suddenly Roshana understands. It's obvious.

'To find Jino,' she says.

Sivalu opens his mouth. His teeth are big and yellow, his gums are black, his tongue is red and wet. 'Let's do that, then,' he says. 'Let's go there.'

Roshana couldn't say how, but it seems they have already set off. She couldn't say where they are going, either, or even in which direction. All she knows is that she is walking, walking quickly, trying to keep up with the jackal as he slinks along in front of her. She is more aware of the motion of his legs than she is of her own. His legs are long, and move so fast they seem to flicker. Roshana has never really watched a four-legged animal hurry before. She is fascinated.

'Here we are, then, Mistress!' says Sivalu suddenly. 'Welcome home!'

Roshana is bewildered. She can't see where they are. Everything is a watery blur.

'Where are we?'

The jackal grins again. 'This is your palace.'

Roshana realizes she is looking at a brick wall, with a large pair of gates set in it. As she follows Sivalu through the gates she recognizes them. They are the gates of Mr Nazeer's shirt factory.

How did they get here, all the way across on the other

side of town? And more to the point, how could Jino have found his way back here? Roshana starts to suspect Sivalu is playing a trick on her. Any minute now he will start jumping up and down and chasing his tail again. He'll roll over on his back and kick his paws in the air, laughing at her.

Everything looks just the same as it did when she lived here. There is the heap of old crates in the corner of the yard, against the wall. Sivalu trots over and starts sniffing them, just like a dog.

And there, alongside the heap of crates, is the little caravan with no wheels.

Roshana wanders up to it.

How small it is, she thinks. How small, and how dilapidated. This dingy corner at the bottom of the yard is the little caravan's last resting place. It will not go from here until it is broken up for scrap. The rain runs in streams down the outside of it and pools on the ground.

The sky is quite dark. It is no longer apparent whether it is still morning or some other time of day or night.

Light shines from the scratched plastic windows of the caravan. As Roshana stands hesitating, there is a muffled sound of someone moving around inside.

The new people.

Roshana feels very peculiar. She looks round for Sivalu, to ask him what to do, but there is no sign of him. The magical jackal has vanished as completely as if he had never been there.

The big umbrella has vanished too, Roshana realizes. She is wet through. She could not be wetter if she had been swimming with all her clothes on.

There is nothing for it now but to knock on the door of the caravan.

Roshana knocks.

She hears footsteps, and the door opens. An elderly little man looks out, staring at Roshana through a pair of thick glasses.

'Another one!' he says.

Behind the little old man appears an equally elderly woman, presumably his wife. She wears a sari of king-fisher blue, faded and patched. She holds the end up over her face. Above the veil, two fierce suspicious eyes contemplate Roshana.

Before anyone else can speak, a voice calls loudly from inside the caravan. It is the voice of a baby, a little boy who is evidently enjoying himself immensely. It is the voice of Roshana's baby brother wanting to know where all the attention has gone.

'Jino!' calls Roshana.

The couple fall back, exclaiming, as the dripping girl leaps up the step and hurtles into the caravan.

The first thing she sees in there is Jino. He is sitting in a high-chair, banging on the tray of it with a big silver spoon. His face is covered in ragi.

'Rosha!' he shouts. 'Rosha! Rosha!'

Roshana pounces on him and snatches him up, hugging him to her, showering kisses on his head.

The second thing she sees in the caravan is an extra-ordinary figure. She is quite short, and quite plump. Her hair has at some point been combed up onto the top of her head, though it's come down since and flops all over her face. She's wearing high-heeled shoes and a Punjabi suit in a pattern of bright pink, yellow and orange. Her trousers are very grubby and splashed with mud. Her shoes used to be white. The heel of one of them wobbles brokenly as she stumbles across the floor and flings her arms round them both, Roshana and her little brother.

'I only borrowed him!' the apparition wails. She seems frightened and aggressive and determinedly cheerful, all at the same time. 'I was going to bring him back tonight!'

Evidently, this is the first her hosts have heard of it. The man gazes glumly at the two young women who have invaded his home and started shouting at each other. His wife, meanwhile, is trying to take her spoon away from the baby, who protests loudly and will not let her, so instead she tries to take Jino from Roshana. Roshana, naturally, clings to Jino, while Smita Anjumbandare clings to her.

Beneath the unruly hair Smita has heaps of make-up on, as always. It is all smeared across her face. She has been crying. The kohl has run down her cheeks like trails left by several sooty snails.

'I can't go home, Roshana,' she whines. 'I'm frightened . . .'

'Come. Come. Come,' clucks the old woman, somewhat frightened herself. She has now decided Roshana's condition is the most immediate problem and has fetched a grey old towel. 'You're half-drowned!' she says reproachfully, diving at her with it.

There is something of a muddle, with everyone talking at once, and baby Jino's aggrieved tones ringing out over the top of it all. Roshana, shivering, reluctantly accepts that she should be dry, or at least less wet, and that nothing can be done about it while Jino is in her arms. She inserts him back in the high-chair, where he sits quite happily sucking a piece of dried pawpaw the old man has given him, and banging his spoon on the tray. While his sister attempts to use the towel, the old couple wrap her first in an unravelling old cardigan and then in a blanket that looks as if someone has been using it instead of a carpet.

For a little while, no one understands anyone else, except perhaps Jino, who comprehends that his beloved sister has come for him, and that he is the centre of all this commotion. Then Roshana manages to get it through to the old woman that she is baby Jino's sister, and that Smita is no relative of theirs at all. 'Her mother works where my mother used to work,' she says as she wipes Jino's dirty face. 'And her sister is my schoolfriend.'

Once the old woman understands that much, she makes the old man understand it too; and then they both glare in a shocked, disapproving way at Smita. She has been hiding here for two days, apparently, pretending to be a young mother cast out by a cruel husband.

'There was nowhere else to go,' she moans, as if that explained or excused anything.

In the high-chair Jino throws himself from side to side, singing at the top of his voice. He has been having a fine time, obviously, being fussed over and played with and fed all sorts of good things.

Smita sits shivering too now, as if in sympathy with Roshana, and smiling at her hosts, oblivious to the trouble and offence she has caused them. 'They are the kindest people in the universe,' she tells Roshana.

Chapter 25

The little man in the glasses brings four cups of strong tea, boiled in a pan with condensed milk and sugar. 'I don't understand,' he keeps saying. 'I don't understand.' He doesn't ask any questions, Roshana notices, so perhaps he doesn't really want to understand.

Roshana thinks, I don't understand either, really. One minute I was dreaming, the next I was back here.

Smita is talking but she isn't making any sense. She sighs, 'Poor Jino,' and smiles a big white smile, and laughs. 'Arun didn't like you, did he? No he *didn't*! Not at *all*!' Roshana sits between them, between her baby brother and his abductress. When Smita tries to reach across to pet him, she leans forward and blocks the way.

The old man tips another spoonful of sugar into his tea and stirs it emphatically. His wife starts to speak but he interrupts her. 'I don't understand,' he says again, determinedly.

Jino chews his spoon, looking unconcernedly from one to other of the faces in the little metal room. His sister gives him a drink from a cup of milk. He blows bubbles in it and laughs. He thinks he is very clever.

For her part, Roshana feels very grown-up, now, and in control. She wants to go home. She puts down Jino's cup and her own. She thanks the caravan's new occupants for their hospitality and, not looking at Smita, apologizes to them for all the trouble they have had. Then she picks up baby Jino and carries him out into the rain.

'Roshana!' Smita lunges from the caravan, clutching at Roshana's arm. Roshana pulls away. She sees the old couple watching doubtfully from the window.

Smita blinks and grimaces through the rain. She appeals to Roshana. 'Roshana! What am I to *do*?'

Bowing her head and doing her best to shelter Jino, Roshana strides away across the yard. 'Go and jump in the river, Smita,' she suggests.

The shirt factory is in total darkness, obviously closed. The rain is as heavy as ever.

Jino starts to complain. After the nice comfortable place where everyone was so good to him, he does not approve of being taken out into the wet and dark. Roshana hushes him, holding on to him tightly.

Outside the gate, the grass grows thick and tall and green. It is running with rain.

Where has all this grass come from? There never used to be so much grass around here.

Roshana turns around.

All the buildings have disappeared. There is only the grass, and in the distance, long low clumps of black that might be trees. Beyond them are vague smudges of blue and purple.

Perhaps they are the hills. Or perhaps they are the sea, standing up in lumps, or the way the end of your pillow looks when you wake up in the middle of the night and can see it only very dimly.

She can't see Jino very well now either, only a dark shape in her arms.

This is still a dream, then. 'I think we'd better keep going,' Roshana tells her little brother.

Jino offers no opinion.

The rain goes on and on.

The road goes up a hill.

'I remember this place,' Roshana says.

Jino struggles briefly. Roshana holds him higher on her shoulder. 'You're very heavy,' she scolds him. 'That's all the ragi you've been eating, you little pig!'

At that, baby Jino makes a snorting noise so very like a pig that Roshana looks carefully at his face, just in case he has changed. It is still Jino, though; she is sure it is.

'Is it the rain?' she asks him. 'Is it the rain making you sneeze?'

As they reach the top of the hill, a long low liquid shadow runs out of the grass. Roshana halts, startled.

'There you are, Mistress!'

It is Sivalu the magic jackal.

'You found him!'

He bares his fangs.

Roshana frowns. If she can keep hold of Jino to the end of the dream, she thinks, then he will still be there when she wakes up.

'I suppose you want paying now,' she says to the jackal, ungraciously.

Sivalu throws back his head and laughs. He starts clowning again, running in circles, snapping at his tail. He seems very happy.

He comes and rubs against Roshana's leg, showing her his throat. He rolls his eyes.

'Give me a kiss,' he says.

It is very white, Sivalu's throat, white as clean linen; white as snow in a storybook.

'I will not,' says Roshana.

Sivalu thinks this is perfectly hilarious. 'A good job I didn't say that to you!' he barks.

Roshana shifts Jino to the other shoulder. 'I didn't *ask* for your help,' she points out.

Sivalu fawns on her again. 'Give me a kiss anyway,' he suggests.

Roshana stoops and kisses his snow-white muzzle.

The stink of him is bad, even in a dream. He smells of blood, old blood: the blood of every dead thing he has ever eaten.

Roshana feels sick. Sivalu is skipping in the rain. 'Bless you, Mistress! May you live forever and have a thousand children!'

Despite herself, Roshana smiles.

She walks on, following Sivalu. Walking now is no effort. She floats through the air.

Sivalu stops. He looks down from the edge of the road, into the valley.

Roshana is starting to be frightened again, for no reason at all. 'What is it?' she calls. 'What's down there?'

She thinks it is a building. It seems to be a white house with a roof of green tiles, and palm trees all around. It is Rajah's house, their house. What it is doing down there, she doesn't know.

'Someone must have moved it.'

She holds Jino up, so he can see too.

'Soon be home,' she tells him.

Then Sivalu starts to howl.

The sound makes Roshana feel dizzy. She is sure he will use up all the air, howling like that. She feels that she must get Jino into that house, urgently, before they run out of air.

Which way? The road divides in two. One road will take them home, the other will only take them on and on, over the hills and into the jungle, where they will be lost forever.

At the fork in the road, someone is standing.

It is a man in a big turban. He is a silhouette, as if day has come and the sun is shining brightly behind him. He is standing with his hands on his hips, waiting for her.

Suddenly, his face is very close. It looks down at her. It is a face like old black leather, wizened and creased.

Hello, Roshana, says the Shadowman.

Roshana's heart is beating fast. She tries to speak. Her lips feel as if they have not been opened for a hundred years, and spiders have woven their webs across them.

What a burden, says the Shadowman. He means baby Jino, in her arms.

When he says that, Jino suddenly becomes incredibly heavy. It is like carrying a big stone.

The Shadowman reaches out one smoky black hand and touches Jino's brow.

Roshana tries to pull away, to put herself between them; but wherever she turns, the Shadowman is there in front of her.

He is so heavy, he whispers. *You can't carry him a step further*.

Roshana hears herself say loudly, 'What rubbish! Of course I can.' She is not sure she believes it, though. She fears the Shadowman may be telling the truth.

The Shadowman stretches out his arms to take the baby. Roshana starts to run. The arms of the Shadowman stretch after her, longer and longer.

Give him to me, he says.

'No!'

The arms of the Shadowman multiply like the arms of Shiva.

Life would be so much easier without him, the Shadowman reminds her. *You said so*.

The Shadowman's arms are the branches of the banyan tree. They wrap themselves around Roshana and Jino. Roshana's neck and legs and shoulders all ache. Dimly she can hear a sound. Is it Sivalu, still howling, or Jino crying? The Shadowman weaves a cage of darkness around them. When it is finished, he will be able to carry them both away to his castle.

The crying comes from overhead. Roshana forces her head between the branches and sees the jackal has shot up to a vast size, like an ogre or a demon. He has planted his four feet at the four corners of the earth, north and south and east and west. He looks big enough to swallow the moon.

He looks down at her through the leaves of the banyan.

Roshana's heart fills with relief and joy. Sivalu will save them.

But even as she looks, a darkness spreads across Sivalu's face. It is like watching the shadow of a cloud flow up the side of a mountain and over the top.

Roshana can't see what's casting that shadow. It is something too big to see. It is still spreading. It spreads to cover Sivalu, to cover the tree, to cover the whole earth.

It is the Shadowman. He is as big as the sky.

He is Night itself.

He is everywhere.

His hand reaches down, down, down to stroke Roshana's cheek. It feels cold and dry as a chill desert breeze.

I think you must give me the boy, says the Shadowman in Roshana's ear.

Roshana loses her temper then.

'Nobody's interested in what you think!' she shouts, 'In case you don't know, you're only a *bad dream*!'

As she shouts, in some way she could never explain, she *sees* her words go shooting up into the darkness. It is as if they had turned into something like a beam of light or a jet of water. Roshana's words pierce the Shadowman as if they were the jet from a hose, and he no more than rotten black cloth stretched thin, like a vast sail. He explodes without a sound into a million billion tiny flakes of blackness that sift down through the air like fragments of burnt paper whirling out of a bonfire.

Baby Jino chokes and coughs. Roshana ducks her head and covers his as the universe tumbles around them in pieces. The pieces are black leaves, black flowers, black feathers. They pelt her like rain. They *are* the rain. Roshana looks up and finds she is sitting on the doorstep of the house, with Jino in her arms.

People are pointing cameras at her again.

Chapter 26

In a moment, the police arrive and push the journalists back. The sharp-faced detective gathers Roshana and baby Jino beneath her cape and rings the doorbell.

Wrapped in her shawl, Amma stands against the wall, swaying but on her feet. She clasps Jino to her and starts to cry.

Summoned from his office in Gabon Street, Rajah comes pounding through the door like an avenging elephant. Relief radiates from him, visible, immense. He scoops up baby Jino and holds him up in the air, triumphantly. 'Safe at last!' he shouts. Then he too bursts into tears. Jino gurgles.

Roshana has a bath. When she starts to undress, she discovers she is still wearing the ancient cardigan the old woman in the caravan insisted on draping around her.

She goes to bed, and sleeps a bit, on and off. She dreams quiet, slight dreams, about drifting boats and silver birds.

That evening, just as they finish supper, there is a ring at the doorbell. It is Mr and Mrs Anjumbandare, with Smita. They have brought her to see Amma and Rajah. It is strange to have her here in the house. Beneath her raincoat she is as dressed up as ever, in a shiny lime green suit, with all her lipstick and lacquer, and pink nail polish. She has stopped chattering, though, and her eyes dart nervously about, as if she has had a great shock and fears that whatever she looks at might make it happen again.

Smita's mother pushes something in front of her, a bundle of scratched white tubes and fabric with little wheels at the bottom, all bunched together. It is baby Jino's pushchair, folded up. Smita's parents look tired and strained, Roshana notices.

Amma and Rajah take their visitors into the front room and close the door, so their conversation won't wake Jino. Roshana is forgotten, left behind among the supper things. Clearing the table, she thinks that she should be getting an apology too. It was her brother Smita took, and she was the one who found him and brought him back.

'Where was he?' the detective had asked her, when Amma and Jino were reunited.

'In the caravan,' Roshana had answered.

'The caravan at the factory? We checked there.' The detective was speaking to Mrs Chowdry rather than Roshana, wanting to impress upon her that the police had done their job properly.

Roshana had decided to say no more about it. When they asked her why she'd gone to the caravan, she shrugged. 'We looked everywhere,' she says. 'Me and my friends.'

If she sits by the door to the front room, she can hear most of what they are saying in there. Smita is saying that the plan came to her in an instant when she spotted Jino in his pushchair, parked under the fire escape. She was on her way to the railway station, where she told Mr Masulkur, apparently, that Jino was another of her many cousins, making his first trip to the city. When she arrived, she told her real cousins that Jino was the child of a sick neighbour and that she was helping to look after him. And when she saw Arun, her ex-boyfriend, she told him Jino was her son.

'He wanted me to marry him,' Roshana hears Smita say. 'I don't want to marry him. I'm not in love with him any more.' Roshana wonders if she will go on to tell them about her new man, the musician who drives a taxi; but seemingly Smita has not yet reached the point of needing to confess everything to everybody, and she continues talking about Arun. 'I was sure if he thought I had a baby that I had been keeping secret from him, he would change his mind about me,' she says. Evidently it worked. 'Men don't want a woman who already has a child,' Smita says firmly.

Roshana smirks to herself. She wonders what Rajah must think of this idea of Smita's.

'Then the rain began,' Roshana hears Mr Anjumbandare say, sadly, 'and Mr Masulkur sent a message to our cousins saying he was going to stay put until it stopped.'

'I was frightened!' Smita says. She sounds almost proud of the fact. 'I didn't know what to do!' What she did, it emerges bit by bit, was snatch up Jino and run to the station, where she screamed and shouted until they let her on the first train that was allowed to leave. By the time they reached the town, Smita had worked herself up into such a state that she was too terrified to bring Jino home.

Sitting alone in the dining room, Roshana wonders why Smita didn't go to the police and tell them she had found him, and give a false name so they couldn't trace her. Smita Anjumbandare is not only a bit mad, she concludes; she's a bit stupid.

At that moment the door opens and they all come out. Smita walks steadily, holding her head up. Behind her Roshana can see Ganesh, smiling from his shrine. Telling her story has obviously calmed Smita down and restored a good deal of her self-esteem, however wicked she has been. She smiles when she sees Roshana, and falls on her knees. 'Roshana! I'm so sorry! You must have been so worried!'

So Roshana receives her apology after all.

'And it was all my fault!' says Smita, passionately. 'You mustn't blame yourself for a moment!'

Roshana can't think of anything to say. Jino is safe and well, and she should forgive the silly woman. The sisters at Blessed Nativity are always talking about forgiving your enemies. But she can't say she forgives her if she doesn't, and she doesn't because she can't; not yet. That's that.

Roshana's eye falls on the pushchair standing against the wall. In her anxiety to leave the caravan, she had forgotten all about it. And nobody, it seems, had dared to remind her.

'Where is the engine?' she asks Smita. 'You lost that, I suppose.'

Smita gets up, looking bewildered. There is a little pause, then everyone starts talking at once. Rajah is asking Roshana what she means, and Amma is saying it doesn't matter, and Smita's father is promising to find baby Jino's engine and bring it back.

Roshana leaves them to it. She runs upstairs to see Jino.

The curtains are closed; the room is very dim. The rain beats ceaselessly on the window. Jino is in his cot, wide awake, as if he senses something special is going on and doesn't want to miss it. He gives a beautiful smile and crows out loud when he sees his big sister come in. He kicks his feet and holds up his arms. Roshana sits on the edge of the bed and plays with him for a while, leaning into the cot to tickle him and talk to him, and walking his chewed old duckling up and down his tummy. She never realized before what a pleasure that is. Jino, of course, is delighted, and shows no sign of getting bored, however often she does it.

After the Anjumbandares leave, Amma comes into the bedroom. 'I must go back to bed, sweetheart,' she groans. 'I feel so *weak*!'

Roshana reaches into the cot and starts to lift Jino out. Amma cries, 'No, Roshi, leave him!', but Roshana takes no notice. Bringing Jino with her, she gets into bed beside Amma. Amma sighs and hugs them both.

Roshana cuddles up to Amma. It is like being a little girl again.

Roshana plays with Jino, who shows no signs of going to sleep. She asks, 'Amma, do you remember Sivalu?'

Her mother yawns. 'Who?'

'In the story.'

'Sivalu?' Amma rubs her eyes. 'He was the wicked creature who stole the princess!' she says.

Roshana frowns. 'Was that it? I don't remember. I didn't think he was wicked.'

She is about to say something more when the door opens again and Rajah comes in. He sees his baby stepson in his bed and smiles a huge smile.

There is a terrible silent moment. Roshana feels a huge, shameful guilt wash over her. How could she ever have suspected her sittappa of wishing to harm Jino, let alone Amma? She must have been dreaming all along.

'I know that story,' Rajah says.

Chapter 27

Rajah sits with the three of them on the bed. It is quite a squash. He folds his hands on his belly and says:

'Once upon a time there was a poor weaver whose name was Jamil. He lived in a shack by the river, a poor shack with holes in the roof and walls. Every time the river rose, it flooded Jamil's shack, and spoiled all the cloth he was weaving, so he had to do it all over again, you see, for no more pay, which made him even poorer.

'Now Jamil the weaver had no money, and no wife, and no shoes, but he had a clever jackal; and his name was Sivalu.'

Amma lies back with her eyes closed and a contented smile on her face, falling asleep really. Baby Jino, in his sister's lap, sucks his fingers and pulls at his toes and contributes his own high-pitched interjections. Roshana watches her sittappa and listens to the story, hearing how the clever jackal procured wonderful gifts for his master: first a suit of fine clothes, which he got by tricking a vain merchant; and then a magnificent palace, by tricking a greedy sultan; and finally the heart and hand of the emperor's beautiful daughter, by tricking nobody at all, but only showing her what was there for all the world to see, that Jamil the weaver was a good man, loyal and generous and true.

Roshana has never heard Rajah tell a story before. He does it really well, with all the different voices. He makes her laugh. When it is done, when Jamil has married the princess and they are living happily ever after in the magnificent palace, Roshana leans over and rewards him, with a kiss.

He smiles at her happily and proudly; and gratefully too, she thinks. 'Good-night, Roshana,' he says.

'Good-night, Amma,' says Roshana. 'Good-night, Appa.' And though it scarcely seems any time at all since she got out of it, she goes to her own bed.

Chapter 28

Baby Jino is fast asleep on his mother's breast. Jyoti is asleep too, sleeping away the last of her sickness. Tomorrow she will be well, Rajah thinks confidently, and things will start getting back to normal. No more journalists, no more detectives. Gently he lifts Jino and gives him a little kiss on his smooth, downy forehead. As he lays the little boy in his cot, he gives silent thanks to the gods that they have all come safely through this bad, mad time.

In her room, Roshana lies on her back, completely relaxed, listening to the rain still beating on the roof. Tomorrow, she will go back to school and see her friends, and everyone will come crowding around, wanting to hear all about how she found her baby brother. Even the nuns will want to know. She is sure they will all be disappointed when they hear how little she has to tell, for she has no intention of saying anything about all the strange things she thought were happening to her at the time, strange, dreamlike things that make no sense when you think about them. She wonders whether Jeevamani will be at school tomorrow, and how she will react to all the trouble her sister has been causing. How awful to have

Smita Anjumbandane as your sister, Roshana thinks, as she turns over and falls asleep.

In his cot, baby Jino sleeps with his mouth half-open. There is a faintly puzzled expression on his face, as though he is trying hard to understand something someone is saying to him. In his little fist, he clutches a shiny black feather.

Do you dare close your eyes?

In the world of Dreamtime anything can happen.
Be careful what you say.
Be careful what you do.
Be careful what you wish for.
Be careful . . .

In Dreamtime, you must look before you leap . . .
Do you dare cross the threshold?

Also in the
DREAMTIME
series

DREAMCATCHER
STEPHEN BOWKETT

There is a secret behind the crumbling factory that
stands alone in the U.S. city of Kenniston. John Doyle
and his streetwise friend Dodger should have found
out more before stepping inside. But welcomed by the
hippies living in the building, given food and shelter,
the boys feel safe . . .

Yet deep beneath the cellar at the dark heart of
the world, the Shadowman is weaving his dreams, and
the powerful ancient forces of the land are flowing
strongly.

SHADOWSONG
JENNY JONES

Everyone thinks the new drama teacher at Gilly's school is a bit strange, but he has encouraged Gilly in her singing and painting. So, when he demands that she paint a mural in his cottage to make up for losing the mask he lent her for the school play, she puts aside her misgivings and agrees to do it.

But why does the cottage look like it's been empty for years? And why does her painting seem to have a life of its own? Who is really interested in Gilly's talents?

ICETOWER
CHRISTOPHER EVANS

Rhys Morgan and Jack Dawson are the last two boys on the school bus. It's the same every day. Suddenly, alone in the bus with the brakes failing, they find themselves plunging down a snow-blasted mountainside. Careering wildly out of control the bus crashes . . .

Into a river and into a different world. A world where crows talk and nothing is what it seems. The world of the *Icetower* and its dark owner. A world where Rhys is going to need super-heroic strength if he is to save Jack – a boy he can no longer trust.